·EVIL CALLED CLEGG

-hunter Percy Clegg is intent on
n Steve Westerley not only for the
due on him in distant Arkansas,
.o because the outlaw killed the girl
·d hoped to marry. On the way
ey are taken prisoner and brought
ranch owned by the dying Rodriguez.
that whilst in the penitentiary,
met Rodriguez's former partner
. him to part with a map leading
old mine containing silver bullion.
·anied by Rodriguez and his sons,
.l to recover the silver, but who
.n alive?

A DEVIL CALLED CLEGG

A DEVIL CALLED CLEGG

by

Tex Larrigan

Dales Large Print Books
Long Preston, North Yorkshire,
BD23 4ND, England.

British Library Cataloguing in Publication Data.

Larrigan, Tex
    A devil called Clegg.

    A catalogue record of this book is
    available from the British Library

    ISBN   978-1-84262-539-2 pbk

First published in Great Britain in 1992 by Robert Hale Limited

Copyright © Tex Larrigan 1992

Cover illustration © Gordon Crabb by arrangement with
Alison Eldred

The right of Tex Larrigan to be identified as the author of this
work has been asserted by him in accordance with the
Copyright, Designs and Patents Act, 1988

Published in Large Print 2007 by arrangement with
Robert Hale Ltd.

Dales Large Print is an imprint of Library Magna Books Ltd.

Printed and bound in Great Britain by
T.J. (International) Ltd., Cornwall, PL28 8RW

For Robin and his woman, who love the mountains and wide open spaces...

One

Clegg stretched his long lean length on the bed, his eyes still closed from sleep. He moved a little and broke wind. The night before had been good and he was full of well-being and gratitude to the girl who'd made it possible. The Deacon had been right when he'd told him that Birdie Firehorse was the best whore in Texas.

He reached for her but the bed beside him was empty. Suddenly every nerve and instinct in his body was twanging as a whisper of movement above him brought his eyes wide open. Above him, in the early morning light was Birdie, bent over him. He grasped her wrist as hand and knife came down unerringly for his exposed chest. He twisted her wrist and she screamed as she dropped the knife.

'You bastard! You didn't tell me you were taking The Deacon in! You're a bloody bounty-hunter!' He saw behind her the clutter of unfolded wanted posters she'd taken from his vest pocket.

He showed his teeth in a wolfish grin and twisted and pulled until she lay under him, her naked shape hard against his own muscled body.

'You didn't ask me. Why should you care? My money's as good as anyone else's.' He frowned, the scar under his right eye showing red. 'What's The Deacon to you?'

'He and my paw were pards. They rode together when I was a child,' she answered sullenly, rubbing her bruised wrist.

'Then your paw weren't no good,' Clegg laughed. 'A feller's known by the company he keeps and The Deacon sure stinks! He'd hold up his own mother for the gold in her teeth!'

Birdie renewed her struggles to escape and in doing so slapped him hard. He slapped her back and she whimpered. She wriggled and he turned her so that she was on top and he had one arm clamped about her as he gathered her two wrists in one hand.

He smelled her womanly scent and leaned up and kissed each bosom savouring her brownish-pink nipples. He bit one lightly and felt it stiffen. It sent a thrill through him even though she'd worn him out the night before.

'If you were a man I'd choke you for what you tried to do. But as it is,' he said thickly, 'I know a better way...' His legs wound about her backside and she could feel his growing hardness.

'Let me go you horny bastard,' she yelled but his hand came up behind her head and he forced her mouth to his. He forced it so hard she bit her own lip and she could taste blood and then he was rolling her over and his thrust was deep and sure.

'I'm warning you, Clegg, I'll make you pay...'

'I'll pay.' He nuzzled her neck below the ear.

'I don't mean in dollars, damn you...' Her eyes closed as she fought to keep her anger against his touch. She missed the narrowing of his eyes as he paused in his caresses.

'How so, then? Going to stick one of your bushwhacker customers on me?'

Her eyes opened wide like a tiger-cat's, no longer turned on by what he was doing to her.

'So you're insulting me now, eh? You think I'm just a cheap...'

'Shut up! Enjoy what you're getting and forget you've ever heard of The Deacon. He's not the same palooka your paw knew. He's got twenty years more of sheer hoss-piss behind him ... or maybe you know that? When was the last time you saw him?'

She stared up at him, her passionate half-Mexican, half-Indian mouth turned down at the corners.

'Five years ago when I was thirteen. He came looking for Paw. He didn't know he'd been shot down by Juarez's volunteers.'

'So you don't know he's wanted in five

States for kidnap and murder and the odd rape, not to mention a couple of piddling bank jobs when he was hard up for ready cash?'

She shook her head. 'I don't know anything about him. I only remember he was kind to me as a child. He once kissed me...'

'I bet he did! He has a liking for young girls. He dresses and acts like a preacher, all sanctimonious unction and a blast of hellfire to impress the Sunday chapel womenfolk.'

'I don't know what sanctimonious unction means but he always liked to preach about hell and damnation and saving souls. When he was drunk, Paw always said he preached the best sermons he ever heard. Really meant what he said. It was only when he was sober he was cold and calculating. Paw said he was most dangerous when he was sober.'

'Is that so? Your paw was one smart feller. I must remember that because he's going to be sober from here on until we reach Fort Smith.'

'Where is he now?'

He looked down at her, a thin smile twisting his lips. She shivered as she looked up at him. It was only curiosity on her part. She would sure hate to have this man hunting her like an animal.

'Why do you want to know? Thinking of setting him free for old time's sake?'

She shrugged. 'Just curiosity. He was kind to me when I was a snotty-nosed kid. Once, when they were both drunk and Paw was going to beat me, he laid into the old man and hammered him. I lit out but I heard him spouting about "suffering little children" or some such crap. He was a great guy when he was drunk.'

'Huh! Maybe I should keep him tied and pissed out of his brains until we reach Fort Smith!'

'From what I hear, he's in no fit state to run!'

'Yeah, well, he's a lucky bastard. I aimed for his balls and took him in the thigh. He'll live to frig and fight in the State pen if Judge

Parker doesn't stretch his neck first.'

'You think he'll hang?'

Clegg shrugged indifferently. 'It ain't my worry. I just haul the bods in. As long as I get my money, I'm satisfied. This sonofabitch is worth ten thousand dollars, so I'm not likely to let him go.'

'That's a lot of dough.'

'Yeh, well he's wanted in five States and you name it, he's done it. Some feller, this psalm-singing old friend of yours. Make no mistake, Birdie, my girl, but this palooka isn't the same feller you knew five years ago. No sir! He's a crap-bag of the worst order. He stinks to heaven and beyond.'

Birdie struggled to free herself and Clegg allowed her to go. When she was standing well away from the bed she had the courage to say softly, 'And you? Are you so very different from The Deacon? I think you're a crap-bag too!'

Clegg threw back his head and laughed. The black hair, streaked with grey fell over his eyes and hid their expression. Birdie

15

relaxed at the sound. He was amused.

'Birdie, you're one smart girl. Do you know they call me Diablo down in Mexico?'

'No, I didn't, but I can believe it.'

'Yeh, but there's one difference between me and that coyote I'm taking back. I get paid for what I do. I get paid by the government. He don't. What he does is for himself. Savvy? I got immunity. He hasn't.'

Birdie gulped. 'I think if we're all done, you can pay me and I'll go. Jewson don't like us girls to hang around the hotel over long when it's daylight. We gotta live after you've come and gone.'

Clegg lay back and watched as she dressed. The low round neck of the grubby white blouse showed off the luscious rounded breasts that had been so exciting during the night. Her long black hair flowed over them like a silky waterfall. For a whore she was surprisingly clean. The red cotton skirt was newly washed and short enough to show firm well-shaped calves. Her ankles were trim and her feet well-cared for.

He liked the smile and the direct look from sparkling black eyes. Yes, Birdie Firehorse was quite a looker early in the morning. Not like some he'd known, who looked stupefied with drink and sleep and smelt like something dropped down the privy.

'It's a pity, you know.'

'What's a pity?'

'That I should leave you behind. What about you lighting out from this dog-shit town?'

'Dog-shit town? What d'you mean, dog-shit? Batuco is an up-and-coming town! Only last year there were three new saloons built and the sheriffs office, and...'

'Stop yakking! You don't know what you're talking about! Batuco means what it says, it's nothing but a goddamn watering hole on the way to more important places. It's just a convenient stop after leaving Abilene for a feller to wet his whistle and dunk his pistle before facing the badlands. How's your nursing skills? Could you look after that buddy of yours?'

17

She stared at him as if she couldn't believe her ears.

'You're joking, aren't you? I've never been twenty miles from Batuco except once when I took the stage to Abilene to try my luck and I nearly got knifed for my pains. The local madam was a bitch! She didn't like competition and as I wouldn't work for her, I came back with this.' She whipped up her skirt and presented a thigh to him. It was marred by a long, thin, white scar.

'Yeh, I saw it last night. Remember?'

'You didn't ask me about it.'

'No, well it wasn't any of my business. Now, it might be.' He grinned. 'I'd pay you and at the end of it, you might find yourself better off up in Fort Smith. Your world is your oyster as someone said. What about it? Isn't it time you improved your status in life?'

'Status? What's that?'

Clegg sighed. 'Chre-ist! You don't know much, do you?'

She bridled. 'I know enough to feed me.

That's all that matters. What is status anyway? A fancy name for my pussy? Mine's all right the way it is. I'm not complaining.'

Clegg was grinning. This kid amused him. He was becoming quite enthusiastic in the idea of taking her along. He'd never offered to tag along with any other woman. He was a loner; he didn't need hangers-on in his profession; he had to be free, to move fast when he had to. He hadn't built up a reputation as a devilish hunter of men by acquiring responsibilities.

Yet now he was cheerfully breaking all his own rules for this chit of a kid, with the round cheeks of an Indian mother and the liquid dark eyes of some Mexican stud. He liked her spirit and her loyalty to a man whom she remembered as some godlike creature who'd protected her from her own father. She tried to knife him for that loyalty. She was also good in bed and he remembered that with pleasure. She would make the nights bearable during the long lonely trek...

'Well? How about it, kid? Are you willing to take a gamble? It's not for keeps, honey, so don't get any wild ideas about locking on kinda permanent. Know what I mean?'

'You mean you just want to use me?' She bristled a little angrily.

'Yeh, you might say that. But wouldn't that be better than a different guy every night?'

She shrugged a bare shoulder as her blouse slipped.

'There's always the chance of meeting a *real* man ... one who might just be the right guy. Anyway, I like variety. No time to be bored.'

'You wouldn't be bored with me, honey. I'd see to that. Then you'd have that old pal of yours to cosset. Keep him out of my hair.'

'What's the matter? Afraid of him? He's good with a gun.'

'Yeh, I'm afraid of him,' Clegg snarled in return. 'I'm afraid I might kill him and he's worth more alive than dead. I aim to buy me a cattle-ranch some day when I find the urge to put my feet up and my arse into a rocking-chair!'

'And The Deacon is going to help you do it?'

'Yeh, why not? Ten thousand smackeroos will go a long way to buying in good stock...'

'Wouldn't you feel any guilt at the thought of profiting by a man's death?'

'Aw, hell, honey, if I was capable of guilt I should have died of it years ago. Don't forget you're talking to the devil...'

Suddenly the bedroom door was slammed back on its hinges and a young breathless deputy leapt into the room. He took a hasty look at Birdie before addressing Clegg.

'You'd better get your arse over to the jail. That bastard you brought in last night has the sheriff holed up with him. The bastard bopped him one when he took in his breakfast and he's threatening to let daylight through him if we don't turn him loose! It's a bloody stand-off!'

Clegg cursed mightily and bounded out of bed, stark bollock naked. The youth's eyes bulged and a dull red flushed his cheeks while his Adam's apple worked up and down.

Birdie grinned. 'Haven't you seen a bare-arsed feller before, Jess? Or am I upsetting you by being here?'

Jess hedged and stuttered. 'I'm sorry, Miss Birdie, I shouldn't have barged in like this and I wouldn't have done if it hadn't been for that feller. He took old Margelos by surprise he did, and now he's got a bump the size of a hen's egg on his head. He wants you quick, Mr Clegg.' Now his voice had lost its nervousness and he gave Clegg all the respect his reputation warranted.

Clegg was already into his trousers and shirt and was snapping on his belts with their famous holsters and rose-wood-handled Colts. He tied down the thongs with practised ease and hauled on his boots. The rest could wait.

'Come on, kid, we'll go and untangle this mess of trouble.' He turned to Birdie. 'Have your answer ready. I'm pulling out after breakfast either with this sermon-spouting spitball or without. It's your choice, kid. Never let it be said I forced you in any way.' His glance was fleeting, his eyes cold. She was free to make up her mind.

Her mind was made up before he stepped out of the door. Where he was, she would be safe. Maybe, just maybe, her star was in the ascendent. Above all, she'd be a dumb broad to stay in what he called a dog-shit town.

Then there was The Deacon. Clegg was wrong about the guy. He must be. It would take some doing to convince her that the tall white-headed pardner of her dead father wasn't the guy she always imagined.

She would ride out with Clegg and prove him wrong and she would take care of The Deacon and maybe provide him with a chance to ride free...

She nodded her head as she came to her conclusions. Both were strong resourceful men, both would ensure she came to no harm. She might as well tag along and hitch a ride towards a successful future. Always providing of course, that Clegg was as clever as he made himself out to be. She would follow along and watch this battle of wills between this devil called Clegg and the larger than life character called The Deacon. She was fascinated. She'd not like to bet on either of them...

Two

There was scorn in Clegg's laughter as he watched both prisoner and sheriff.

'And how far do you think you're going to get before I catch up with you?' he lazily asked the guy reclining on the bed, one leg stretched out, the other touching the ground. He was white and drawn, grey grooves etched about his mouth and he looked to have lost weight. But his dark eyes glittered with stubborn life under the grey eyebrows and the shock of white hair bristled aggressively. And the hand holding the gun on the apprehensive sheriff was unerring, and that was what counted.

Sheriff Margelos swallowed and then appealed to Clegg.

'For Chrissakes, Clegg, do something. It's not some bloody joke being stuck here with a madman!'

Clegg shrugged. 'Whose fault's that, Sheriff? I warned you that the bastard was leery. You should have sent this young punk in with his grub. It wouldn't have mattered how long they stayed together!' He grinned as he saw Jess's reaction and the scowl that followed.

'Mr Clegg, that was uncalled for. I'll have you know...'

'Shuddup, Jess, and go and spit somewhere else.' Sheriff Margelos howled him down while The Deacon bit into a chaw of tobacco. There was the click of a Colt being cocked.

'Sheriff, you stop your squawking. I kinda object to earsplitting noises when I'm sober. They turn me real mean.' The Deacon slowly turned his attention on Clegg. 'Howdy, man. Now as to your question, I don't know the answer to that until we try it. How about it, Clegg? A run for it or else two dead men and you with a hole in the gut?'

Clegg laughed. 'What's the matter? Are you piss-proud? I'd get you before you shoot the sheriff here.'

The Deacon looked at him consideringly. 'I don't think you've got my measure, Clegg. Sometime, I'd like to try you out, eyeball to eyeball, no backshooting for us...'

'So you're backing down because of your wound? Very sensible, I'm sure...'

'No, I'm not backing down, Clegg, I'm just preparing to be on my way!'

'You what?' Clegg showed surprise. The feller was loco after all. He must be delirious or some such. 'Now look here...'

The Deacon smiled an icy confident smile and for a moment Clegg went cold. What the hell...? Then he heard the click of a gun behind him and he turned in a crouch, his hand blurring as he went for his Colt. But he was too late; the shotgun blasted and the shot scattered skywards as Birdie Firehorse couldn't resist dragging on the trigger. Clegg's action had panicked her. Her intention had been to just watch what was happening. But seeing the sheriffs shotgun racked up on the wall had given her the idea of holding up Clegg and letting The Deacon go free.

The sight of The Deacon, so little changed, had brought all her memories of him tumbling back. If she was to leave Batuco, she'd rather do it with The Deacon than that devil, Clegg, even though he was good in bed.

Besides, she owed The Deacon a favour. He'd saved her from a beating.

But now, The Deacon was cursing as the sheriff hurled himself backwards and on to the bed to escape the shotgun loads, and his shot-up thigh was taking the strain. He had no interest in what was happening outside the barred cell. Jess was whimpering, having caught a pellet in the cheek, while Clegg dived on Birdie and straddled her. Then he was slapping both cheeks with vigour and seemed to enjoy the doing of it.

'You little bitch! I've a good mind to take you along in irons!' He grasped her shoulders and proceeded to shake her so her head bounced off the floor.

'Don't! Please don't hit me any more! I

never meant to pull the trigger. You frightened me when you fell into a crouch. It was
your fault!' The tears burst from her and she
sobbed.

'Let the kid alone,' growled The Deacon.
'What she says is true. You turned on her
and you could have killed her if she hadn't
blasted that shotgun. You're obscene, man.
Let her get up.'

'Who the hell are you to tell me what to
do?' But Clegg unwound himself from the
slight body and stood up and then held out
his hand to the girl.

She ignored him and staggered upright
under her own steam, her head averted. He
shrugged.

'Have it your own way. Now, you, mister,
just keep your thoughts to yourself, and you
sheriff, get your arse out of there and don't
flirt with danger no more!'

He managed a grin as the sheriff came out
of the cell in a rush giving The Deacon a wide
berth, but The Deacon was busy rubbing his
leg and gritting his teeth. It looked as if the

sheriff had k.o.'d him for the present.

Clegg looked on with no satisfaction. 'It looks as if you're running nowhere, buddy-boy. But you're riding out of this dog-shit town in a wagon in shackles before the sun goes down even if I've got to saw that damn leg off myself!' Then looking from the flustered sheriff and the young deputy, he hitched his gunbelt before nodding at Birdie.

'Watch that little hell-cat, Sheriff. She's got more tricks in her than a mountain-cat's got worms! I'm off to find some breakfast and after that, I'll take that feller off your hands.'

He walked out and slammed the door behind him, still furious at Birdie. The stupid little bitch! She could have got them all killed with her fooling around. He still felt the crawl of fear up his spine as he'd swung round on her. Only he knew how near she had been to death. It was only his disciplined mind that eased his finger from the hair-trigger that saved her. He hawked and spat in the dust. Well, he was a sucker.

His little dream that she might ride along with them, over. The little schmuck didn't deserve to get on in the world. She would always be a cheap little hustler...

'Clegg! I want to talk to you!' He paused, Birdie's urgent call made him wonder what she could want to talk about. He waited for her and sullenly rolled a smoke while he waited. He couldn't help but admire her lilting walk, her bare feet and the way she swayed from side to side. He remembered the body curled about his during the long night hours...

'Yes? What is it? I didn't think you and I had anything else to talk about.'

'Look, let bygones be bygones. I want to ride out with you.'

'Why? So that you can blast me again?' He drew in smoke and then coughed. Hell! She was upsetting him too early in the morning.

'No. That was a mistake, truly it was. I've been thinking and you're right. It's time I moved on from this dump.'

He half-smiled. 'You believe me then? It's

a dog-shit town?'

'Something like that. Then there's The Deacon. I'm sorry for him, Clegg. He's in a bad way although he talks tough. I want to see you don't kill him on the way to Fort Smith.'

'You don't need worry about that. He's worth ten thousand dollars. Is a feller going to pass up that kind of money?'

'But you would get paid whether he's alive or dead!'

'Yeh, but only from one State. I'd only pick up two thousand from Arkansas. If he's hanged or sent to the pen I can claim the extra from another four States. I'm not likely to cock-up on that.' He grinned. 'If you think I'm going to go soft on you and give you a stake, you're mistaken.'

'You said you would pay me...'

'Yeh, for services rendered at the going rate.'

'And for looking after The Deacon?'

'Yeh, that too. It would come out of the bounty.'

'Well, if the offer is still open I'll settle for that.'

'Done. Now do you want to eat?'

'If you're paying!'

'Come along then.' And he put a hand around her slim waist, and looked down at her, the top of her head barely reaching his shoulder. She was a small packet of goods, but by God, she was spunky. It was going to be an interesting trek back to Arkansas. It meant he wouldn't have to fight those frustrating night dreams when he'd been without a woman for a long while...

She was a good trencher. She ate a steak big enough to feed a drover, with all the trimmings of fried eggs and potatoes. Cavorting all night certainly gave her an appetite. Maybe he'd better get extra rations in. He didn't want her to go sour on him. He and his prisoner could tighten their belts but not the little lady if it kept her purring contentedly.

She left him straight after her breakfast to pack her duds, and he visited the store to buy his wherewithals and extra ammo. He couldn't be too careful. The Deacon was the most dangerous and resourceful quarry he'd hunted for years and he wasn't going to make a balls-up of it at this late stage. It had taken six months to catch him, and if it hadn't been for the guy called Buckmaster he could still be hunting him.

He remembered Buckmaster with respect. He was an Indian-lover; a guy who'd lived with the Apache; a guy who'd got him made into a blood-brother of the Apache too.

He smiled as he went about his business in the store. Little Elk, the son of the Apache chief – he wondered what both of them were doing now. The young Indian was probably taking over his particular Apache tribe as his father grew too old and infirm to control the young dog-soldiers who were bent on counting coup.

As for Buckmaster, he grinned when he thought of Belle Nightingale, the tasty madam of the Bird of Paradise cathouse way back in Abilene. He wondered if she was the madam Birdie had had her run in with. It didn't sound like the generous Belle. One thing was sure, Buckmaster would have to watch himself, or he'd wake up one morning, hog-tied. The last time he'd encountered them, it had been a battle of wills between the pair. He remembered Buckmaster paddling Belle's arse with relish...

He had already negotiated a battered old Conestoga wagon and four mules from the livery boss. Now he tossed in extra blankets, another barrel of water and an assortment of bandages and medicines. He didn't want The Deacon cocking his fancy riding boots before they got to Fort Smith. The main reason wasn't the loss of good dough but that they had a long way to go and the body would smell like a travelling shit-house two days after it stiffened. Then they would have problems with flies...

He looked over the mules with satisfaction. A rare team; one salvaged from a burned out way-station and sold to the livery boss by a passing-through drifter who had no use for mules but wanted cash badly to turn into raw liquor.

Birdie was waiting with her carpet-bag when he drove the rig back towards the jail. He stopped.

'Climb aboard. You look worried.'

'I am. Suddenly I don't know whether I'm doing right. I'll be safe with you, Clegg?'

'Safer with me than many I know; that bastard down in the jail for one.'

Birdie pulled down the corners of her mouth. 'Why do you call him so? He's done nothing to you.'

'I been hunting him for six months and back-trailing him means I hear things. He's got a bad reputation, Birdie. He's got no halo hovering over his head. For instance, when I caught up with him, he'd drugged a young girl by the name of Rosalie Neuman. Gave her opium without regard of whether she might become addicted.'

'I don't believe you!'

'You'd better! It was done so that a syndicate could control her father. It was high finance amongst the cattle barons who run the beeves, their rustler friends and the canners way back east. You can check it out by telegraph to Buckmaster. Anyone will tell you about him. I don't *have* to convince you, Birdie.'

She sat beside him, sullen, her hands knotted tightly together. He picked up the reins. The mules were restive.

'Well? Do you want to change your mind? You're free to come or stay in this dog...'

'Yes, I know what you think of this place.' She looked about her and sighed. 'You're right. It is a dog-shit town. I'm willing to take a gamble and it isn't just because The Deacon is coming along. It's time I had a change, but...' She looked sorrowful and Clegg slapped her on the shoulder.

'Cheer up, kid. Even the chickens feel a bit sorry when they first leave the egg! But they soon get used to the change.'

Her sullen mood changed and she gave a reluctant smile.

'You're a funny feller, Clegg.'

'Thank you. It's the first time I've been called funny. So you've made your mind up?'

'Yes. But I wish you wouldn't speak so badly about ... about him.' She nodded towards the jail as they came to a stop in front of it. Clegg shrugged.

'Just as soon as you learn not to be taken in by his charm. On this trip you're my woman, not his, so remember it.'

'And afterwards, Clegg?'

'Ah ... that is when our contract ends. God knows what will happen then. You'll be wanting to make an impression in Fort Smith.' He grinned. 'The soldiers pay well...'

'Christ! Must you always talk like that? Money isn't everything, Clegg!'

'Well now, you could have fooled me! I thought everyone's ambition was to make themselves a good bankroll. Haven't you got ambitions, girl?'

'Yes, but they obviously aren't the same ambitions as yours.'

Clegg laughed and secured his reins, then

swung down in front of the jail. Birdie watched the lean hard figure move inside, with a certain sadness in her eyes.

He was soon back again and this time the sheriff and young Jess were humping The Deacon who had a couple of grey blankets folded on his chest. They heaved him inside the wagon on a makeshift bed that rested on two stout wooden boxes. He looked pale and gritty-jawed and the slightest of groans escaped his lips as he was flung down on the bed.

Birdie sat still, hurting inside for the treatment meted out to the guy she'd remembered over the years as the kindest man she'd known. It was better not to anger Clegg by fussing over him. There was a long way to go yet. Maybe she could ease his suffering later.

Leaving town had been something of a disappointment. Birdie sat morose, fearing she'd done the wrong thing in entrusting herself to the long haul to Arkansas. The

Deacon too had been something of a let down. He'd looked at her with painfilled eyes and said laconically when she'd asked him, 'Yeh, I remember you. Old Tomaso's daughter. Treated you badly because you were half-Indian. Birdie, isn't it?' His cold grey eyes did not soften. Birdie felt chilled. Maybe Clegg had been right after all. He wasn't the same man.

She shivered and thought of the near future bleakly. In her present state, she didn't know whether she could trust either man. At least Clegg had treated her decent when he'd paid for a night with her.

She smelt of horses. Clegg had advised dressing in men's clothes, pointing out the dangers of travelling into the unknown. She'd considered cutting her hair but it was long and lustrous and she always reckoned it was the most beautiful part of her. She would need the influence of that hair if and when she ever reached Fort Smith and beyond.

Her buckskin jacket and leggings had belonged to the stable-lad. She'd swiped them as he lay in a drunken stupor on the straw in the barn. Serve the fool right, she thought viciously; he should have been up and about his work instead of sleeping off a binge just because a bunch of wild drovers had hit town.

Her hair was bundled under a dirty grey stetson. She didn't know the owner. He must have been one of the drovers for it was laid convenient and it sure wasn't young Dirk's.

Now she huddled down, trying hard to look like a boy. She had no gun and she daren't ask Clegg if she might carry one. She didn't quite like it when he raised those strong expressive eyebrows of his. She came to the conclusion she was a little frightened of both men. She glanced back into the wagon to check her carpet-bag was safe. All she had in the world was in that bag. Her small bankroll was hid in a pouch under the check shirt Clegg had given her. At least he was thoughtful. She felt vulnerable. Alone.

She found The Deacon's eyes on her.

Thoughtful. Considering. She smiled and he glowered, turning his head away and closing his eyes. Then his words came softly. 'I could use a drink.'

'There's water in the butt. I'll get you some.'

'No, I want whiskey. I've got a throat like lizard skin.'

'But it's not good for you in your condition. You'd be better with water.' She turned to climb into the wagon but Clegg reached for her arm. He jerked his head at his prisoner.

'Give him what he wants. There's a bottle back there in my possibles bag. One snort, mind you. No more. Comfortable?' He smiled briefly but his eyes did not light up. He was watchful, careful, like a cougar ready to spring any which way. She nodded.

'Back aches a bit. This wagon isn't exactly sprung good, is it?'

His lips twisted. 'You're lucky you're not forking a horse.'

'Where's yours?'

'Swopped it in part exchange for this rig. Gotta get this feller back alive.'

Birdie's face muscles hardened. Suddenly she had a taut feeling of dread. This was going to be no quiet meandering into wide open acres with time to gaze and wonder with awe at Mother Nature. Even if they never met another soul, there was going to be this watchful tension every damn foot of the way. She knew instinctively that once The Deacon's wound was half-way healed, it would become a battle of wits. He'd made an effort already probably knowing he couldn't pull it off but his pride had been assuaged. He'd tried.

She scrambled back into the wagon and found the whiskey and a tin mug and slopped some into it. The Deacon raised himself on one elbow and eagerly snatched it and drank it down in one gulp. He sighed with relief.

'What about another?'

She shook her head. 'He said one and no more.' She glanced at Clegg's rigid back, his attention on the mules and the rough passage.

'Go on,' he whispered. 'If you're quick he'll never know.' The creak of the wagon and the squeak of harness muffled their speech.

'No. Please, it isn't good for you. I'll change your bandage.'

'You're on his side, aren't you? He's paying you well for all the little attentions you give him. Is that it?' He flung the tin mug hard at the arch of canvas opposite. It bounced back and hit the floor of the wagon.

Clegg looked over his shoulder at Birdie.

'Is he giving you a hard time, Birdie? You did right to heed what I said. I don't like being disobeyed. Remember that, girl.'

Birdie swallowed and looked from one to the other. The Deacon smiled at her and it was evil.

'Go on, cuddle up to him and lick his arse if he wants it.'

'What about your bandages?'

'To hell with them! This bloody wound will heal whether you change the bloody bandages or not! Once I get back on my feet...'

'You talk too much, Westerly,' Clegg's voice rang out. 'One of these days we're going to have a showdown.'

'It can't come too soon for me!'

'Or me. I swear when we get a half-day's ride to Fort Smith, I'll trounce you to within an inch of your life!'

'Oh? And why should you feel so ill-fired crazy to do that, or do you do that to all those you bring in?'

'No,' drawled Clegg and suddenly there was a well-used Colt in one hand while the reins were in the other. He turned and cocked the weapon, and it was almost at the middle of his prisoner's chest. 'Only those who've hurt me or mine in the past. You're special, Westerley. You remember a bible-bashing family way back in Idaho, a schoolmaster and his wife and two sons and a daughter? You raped Molly and you killed

45

her brothers when they caught you at it. You were staying with them. You were supposed to be bringing the church to Twofork Creek but you brought misery and death. You killed the parents before you rode away with the gold they had hidden under the floor-boards. Gold they'd worked hard for an' saved towards making Twofork Creek into a God-fearing community. You remember?'

The Deacon's face was white and drained, his eyes shifty, his mouth tight.

'I admit nothing, Clegg.'

'There's a wanted poster for that, Westerley.'

'Posters can lie!'

'Not in this case, Westerley. I was there a week after it happened. I'd come home to the girl I'd pledged to marry and I've been hunting you ever since.'

'You won't believe this, Clegg, but I didn't set out to rape that girl...'

'Pull the other leg, Westerley. I know exactly what happened. Your sanctimonious front cracked and you couldn't resist an innocent God-fearing girl!'

'I tell you...'

'Stow it, Westerley. I don't want to listen to your snivelling explanations. Don't forget I saw the state of the last girl you violated, Rosalie Neuman. You drugged her with opium. Another poor girl who would have gone the same way as Molly, if I hadn't caught up with you. One thing about you, Westerley, they can only hang you once. It's a bloody pity, but it's true. So shut your mouth and be glad you've got some time left. And don't think to influence this kid here into doing something foolish. For next time I aim at you, I don't mean to miss. You'll die without your balls!'

That night they camped in a small draw with plenty of brushwood for a fire.

There had been little conversation after the showdown. Birdie was subdued. She had been shocked at the disclosure. She was tired and dispirited. The Deacon lay on his hard bed and when the meal was ready accepted it with ill grace and little to say.

47

Clegg busied himself in oiling and cleaning his guns, taking care to have both his Colts and his Winchester within range whatever chore he went on to do. Continually he watched the skyline in the dry gulley. It was a dried out river-bed and at each side coarse scrub had grown up and died from lack of moisture. Small cliffs reared up on both sides as the water over thousands of years had carved its way through. But now it would flow only during freak rainstorms. Birdie watched uneasily as he continually raked the rimrock above.

'What is it you're afraid of?' she burst out at last.

Clegg was hunkered down putting on more wood for the night was growing chill. Flames leaped high and his face outlined with black shadows suddenly took on that of a devil. His glance was sardonic.

'We're entering the badlands. We're cutting corners and lopping off time to get to Fort Smith in good time. To do it, we must pass through some high country ... where many of the outlaws hang out. You know what that means?'

They both heard Westerley laugh. Then his voice came loud and clear.

'Friends of mine, don't you forget, Clegg. Friends do you hear? Your life won't be worth hoss-piss if they get within sniffing distance of our fires!'

'You're forgetting something, Westerley,' and now Clegg was smiling with savage malevolance, 'I'm a blood-brother of the Apache. Anyone hurts me, hurts the Apache. But I don't go for showdowns, Westerley. I have my own methods and my own peculiar little ways of getting my prisoners back to base!'

Birdie listened to the exchange. Again she shivered. She hadn't thought of being stalked on the trail when she'd decided to throw in with Clegg. She made up her mind to stay mighty close to Clegg, to hold her tongue and please the cold killing bastard. He was her means of survival. She would endure uncomplainingly; do whatever he wanted, and in the end put one foot on that ladder of success she'd heard so much talk about.

Someday she was going to be somebody who mattered. She would have other people to do her dirty work and as for men ... she would have them drinking out of her slippers!

Three

They had been moving along at a slow back-breaking pace for three days. The terrain was becoming rough and several times Clegg had to get down and guide the lead mules, cursing and straining at every step and the old wagon creaked and groaned as if it would finally collapse. But the wagon bed was strong and built for heavy duty.

There was little talking and Birdie found that Clegg was too tired at night to do anything but curl up in his blankets and snore. She was disappointed. She'd expected him to be virile and exciting and she felt let down. It wasn't often she'd slept alone and she found it a lonesome thing, especially in this wild and lonely land.

She was worried about The Deacon, who lay with his face to the canvas wall and rarely opened his eyes. His wound smelt bad but he wouldn't allow Birdie to tend it. He only grunted impatiently when she offered to help him. Clegg helped him from the wagon each time they stopped for him to relieve himself. Then, he would shrug himself from Clegg's grasp and lean on the wheel of the wagon while he did what he had to do. It was as if pride kept him going, but he hated Clegg's help. Clegg would shrug and walk away and it was Birdie who helped The Deacon back into his bed.

But on the third night The Deacon collapsed. He gave a little moan and slumped into a heap. Birdie, busy teasing a small fire into something fit to boil coffee and fry bacon, heard him go down. At once she was by his side. She was frightened at his pallor. He was completely out.

She called Clegg who was feeding and watering the mules.

'Clegg, something's happened to Mr Westerly.' Clegg raised his head sharply. The "mister" bit always riled him. The man didn't rate respect and the stupid girl would not learn.

'Watch him, he's shamming. He's got something in mind!'

'No, he's clean out. We'll have to lift him back into the wagon.'

Clegg sighed. He was becoming a regular bloody nurse for this guy and he didn't like it. Ten thousand dollars wasn't going to be too much for the humping of him through Indian territory. Why, they didn't even have fast horses but only these mules. If they were spotted, then the wagon and that crowbait of a feller was going to slow them down, never mind having the girl along. On reflection, he now thought he was mad to take her on. His nights had not been improved by knowing she was within feet of him, and him not able to take advantage. He spat. Chre-ist! His eyes had been bigger than his belly where she was concerned.

He moved alongside and looked down at the man. He sure did look a goner, and that riled his already simmering temper. If he died, he would be doing it on purpose to rob him of the extra bounty as well as make a shit-smelling nuisance of himself. No bounty-hunter chose to tote a corpse over hundreds of miles in hot weather; unless that is, he was frightened of the varmint and a dead 'un hurt no one but by the smell.

'Jesus wept!' he said furiously and hunkered down to examine the inert body. Thankfully The Deacon was still alive. Clegg let out a sigh.

'It seems as good a time as any to have a look at that there wound of his.' Birdie went white as Clegg slit the trouser-leg with his Bowie knife and the full stench of the wound hit her nostrils. Clegg himself turned his head and for the first time realized what this man must have gone through. Birdie stared at Clegg furiously.

'It's your fault he's like this. He should have been in a bed with a doctor looking after him. How long is it since you shot him?'

Clegg shrugged.

'Maybe three weeks. He was in bed for a week before we started out. The doc who tended him said he was well enough to travel.'

'And I suppose you shoved him on a horse?'

'Yeh, fastened him belly-down until we reached Batuco. He was gagged too. I wasn't travelling with him yelling his head off, I can tell you.'

'So, you're killing him slowly. You think he'll last until you get him to Fort Smith and you'll ensure he'll die anyway, even if the judge gives him life!'

'Hey, now, just a minute, you've got it wrong. I never thought he was in this state! He stinks pretty bad, but don't we all? He didn't want you to help him so I figured he was on the mend. He's a lucky bugger really. He moved as I shot him. He should have got the lot in the balls, not in the fleshy part of his thigh.'

'Well, if nothing's done now, he's going to die. What then?'

'Oh, to hell! I suppose we'll have to do something. What d'you say?'

Birdie lifted her shoulders. 'Look, mister, I'm no expert. You're the one with the know-how. I can clean a wound and bandage it, but I shudder to think what's under those bandages!'

'Well, now, there's only one way to find out.' Quickly Clegg cut away the sodden scarlet rags and then they both peered down at the bloody mass. The flesh around the wound was red and angry and the rest was just a yellow suppurating cavity that oozed as the bandages were peeled off. Clegg took one look at it. 'There's only one thing to be done. It will have to be cauterized.'

Birdie gasped. She'd never seen a wound cauterized but once she'd heard a man scream in the doctor's surgery way back in Batuco and she didn't want to hear that scream again.

'Must you? Isn't there any other way?'

'We could clean it and wrap it up and take bets whether he would survive. This way's the best. It'll make a mess of his thigh muscle but he's got a better chance to live long enough to hang. We'll do it while he's out. He'll never know what hit him. Get that fire going. I'll use a branding iron I've got in the wagon.'

Soon the flames were leaping high and there was a good bed of red ash in which to thrust the iron. Birdie trembled as if with ague. Clegg watched her shrewdly. The kid was bearing up well for one so young. She was a tough little lady. Lady? Now that word was a funny one to come to mind seeing what she was. But Clegg was fair. She'd gone up in his estimation. She was loyal and forthright, even wrong but she stuck to her opinions. A man could respect a woman for that. Not like some women who agreed with every damn thing a man uttered and then buggered off and left him as soon as someone better came along. She'd not even cast doubts on his manhood, like some women he knew would have done just because he slept alone...

Birdie brought blankets and they laid Westerley on them near the fire and then one on each side; kneeling beside him, they looked at each other.

'Look, if it's too much for you, get yourself away,' Clegg said casually as he waited for the iron to heat to a white-hot glow.

'I'll stay. He might awaken and start thrashing about. You might need my help.'

'Just as you like,' he grunted, 'but I'm warning you it's nothing like barbecuing a steak!'

'I know. I'm not an idiot.'

'Right! Then this is it!'

Suddenly everything was happening together. There was the stench of burnt flesh, a seeming corpse galvanized into shrieking life, a couple of gunshots aimed a little too close and four mules kicking up their heels on their holding lariat and threatening to burst loose.

'What the hell...?' Clegg looked up to see a tall thin Mexican garbed in ragged trousers and poncho and a short, fat, round ball of a man whose sombrero reminded Clegg of a lid on top of a honey jar.

The little man was smiling as both men walked forward. They were confident. They had to be, seeing they had four others on horseback behind them. Clegg cursed. The little drama they had been through had allowed the bastards to sneak up on them and even give two of them time to tie up their horses. The men smelt of garlic and sweat and chili.

'What goes on here then, amigo?' The short one poked The Deacon with his toe. He'd fainted again and was now laid with his wound steaming and blackened.

'What the hell d'you think we're doing,' Clegg growled. 'Who are you anyway?'

The little fat one looked pained. 'I thought everyone knew of the Domingo gang. We're just up from New Mexico.' He grinned. 'I'm worth more than he is,' and his thumb jerked in the direction of his tall partner.

'What about them?' Clegg asked. He nodded slightly in Birdie's direction and motioned to The Deacon's wound.

With trembling fingers she unwound the bandages she'd dug out of her carpet-bag and the mixture of juniper and garlic powder she carried in a small leather pouch.

'What's that?' Clegg asked, one eye on the two standing watching the proceedings.

'A mixture of ground herbs that my mother taught me to use,' she answered. 'I'm going to sprinkle them on the wound before wrapping it.'

'Will they keep the wound clean?'

'I hope so. I've nothing else.'

Clegg nodded. 'Then make a good job of it. I've got a funny feeling...' He stopped and gazed up at the men. He was in the worst possible position to be caught in, crouched on his knees. But they were not acting like they ought to. They were looking at each other. Then both smiled at Clegg.

'You a doctor?. Or is she healing woman?'

'Well...' He saw the sudden doubt in both men's eyes. He hastily changed the words he was about to utter. 'I'm more of a horse-doctor and she's my helper. You haven't answered my question. What about those hombres back yonder?' He nodded to the silent four on horseback.

The little man, who acted like the leader, shrugged. 'They do anything I tell them. Anything. Savvy my meaning?'

'Sure. The heavy muscle mob. Must be re-assuring to have someone else do your dirty work.'

Domingo scowled. 'I assure you, señor, I am quite capable of doing my own dirty work, but when hiring dogs, one doesn't bark oneself!'

The tall thin stranger looked impatient. He glanced at the watching men and spoke quietly and furiously at Domingo.

'Quit fooling around, Domingo, and take these two back to Rodriguez. You want the old man to live, don't you?'

Domingo's face changed. For a moment, vicious satisfaction gleamed from the piggy eyes and then a look of mock sorrow suffused the round, whiskered face.

'Carlos, what a question! Of course I want

him to live.' He shook his head hopelessly as if it was already too late. 'I have been Rodriguez' segundo for twenty years. He is like a padre to me. I know him better than anyone...'

'Better than his sons?' Carlos's tone was mocking.

'Si ... better than Pietro or Marco. Do you doubt that?' His question was harsh; his tone rough and bitter. Carlos appeared to back off and Clegg watched, interested.

There was no doubt about it, there was some kind of black treachery afoot. All was not as it seemed.

'Who's Rodriguez? And is he the one you want us to tend? I'm not sure if we have the time. We're on a long haul to Kansas.' No need to mention Fort Smith or bounty-hunting. Instinctively Clegg knew that these men wouldn't think kindly of bounty-hunters.

'We're not asking you, señor, we're taking you along.' And now there was steel in Domingo's voice. Suddenly there was a useful-looking gun in his hand and trained at Clegg where it would do the most good. Behind him, Clegg heard the cocking of four rifles. He shrugged and came to his feet with his hands well to the front and away from his own weapons.

Domingo's eyebrows came together when he saw the two strapped-down Colts.

'A gunman, eh? You've other interests as well as horse-doctoring.' Then he motioned to Birdie. 'Your woman, I guess?'

Clegg nodded laconically. 'And I aim she stays that way.'

Domingo laughed showing yellow broken teeth between thick lips surrounded by the best set of whiskers he'd seen for many a day.

'Well said for an hombre that's just been made a prisoner of Domingo! Here, Pietro and Marco, get that wagon started up. We'll leave this carrion behind. He looks dead anyway. I don't know why you bothered to brand him unless you did it for fun. What did he do, try for your woman?'

Clegg looked at the man with loathing.

'I don't go anywhere without him.' The two men glared at each other. It was Domingo's eyes that finally broke away. He glanced at Carlos and Clegg went into a crouch and went for his righthand gun. Carlos paused in the act of reaching for Clegg's weapons, his hands instinctively raised. His fingers twitched.

Clegg's slug gauged dirt up between Domingo's boots. He stared down at his feet and then at Clegg, his face pasty grey. Clegg smiled.

'You're lucky. I usually aim for the balls. But I'm wanting no trouble. I'll help this Rodriguez feller if I can and then we'll be on our way. No hard feelings, eh?'

Domingo looked furious, but Pietro and Marco stepped down from their horses. Marco, obviously the elder of the brothers was hard-faced, challenging as he faced Domingo.

'We want to ride. It's our father who's lying bleeding to death and if this man is some kind of a doctor, it makes sense to get him along voluntarily. I say take him along and then let him go...'

'But he'll know our hideout. Do you want that? Don't you hombres ever use your brains?'

'You heard him. He's passing through. He's not interested in us. But he will be if you don't stop acting like some goddamn general!' Domingo's eyes flashed with temper.

'I am the generalissimo of this outfit! I have been for years since your father went soft in the head!'

'You call him soft because he stopped robbing and raiding to build up a good cattle ranch? How many times must we tell you that all that is in the past? Mister, we're asking you to come along with us to see our father. My brother and our men will see you are not harmed and you will be escorted back to the trail when our father is healed.'

'And what if he dies? I'm no miracle worker and neither is she,' nodding to a silent Birdie who was assessing all the men for reasons of her own.

Marco shrugged heavy shoulders. 'Then it is the will of God. He is very sick but he should have a chance, and by the look of this man here, he has more chance of living than he has. Will you come?'

Clegg moved easily, his mind swiftly assessing the situation. It could only take a few days and then when they moved out, they would probably get these men's protection part of the way over the Staked Plains.

'Do you promise to escort us well on our journey?'

'To our boundaries. We can guarantee your safety until then. After that, it is up to you.'

'Right. Then lift my friend aboard the wagon and we'll be on our way.'

The trail was devious, through arroyos and small innumerable canyons until Clegg was lost. He'd tried to keep some kind of landmark clear in his mind, but whether it was deliberate or not, he found himself bewildered as to direction or number of miles they traversed. He only had one clue. Most of the time they travelled east but on the second day they turned due south and up into higher ground. They were now making the perilous journey high into the mountains and it took two of them to manage the mules. Twice The Deacon fell from his makeshift bed and the second time brought him round with a groan and a scream.

'What the hell's happening?' he managed to mutter. Birdie crouched beside him.

'We're being taken up into the mountains by a Mexican by the name of Domingo.'

'Christ! Is he still on the go? He's a vicious little bastard! He crossed my path years ago down in Mexico. Segundo for an old devil called Rodriguez. No doubt the old man's dead...' The Deacon shut his eyes wearily and tried to move his leg. He groaned.

'It's because of Rodriguez we're being taken up into the mountains,' Birdie whispered.

The Deacon's eyes flew open.

'The hell it is!' He gave a half-smile and

then his mouth twisted in pain. 'What the blazes have you done to my leg? It burns as if it is in the fire!'

'Clegg cauterized it. He saved it for you, Mr Westerley. Gangrene was setting in. You're lucky to still have it!'

'So I have to thank him for that too, eh? Not satisfied in trying to blow it off but he must put me through this. I think I should have rather died...'

'Don't be silly! You're talking like a petulant child!'

'I don't want to thank him for anything.' He smiled again. 'Maybe I can turn the tables. I know old Rodriguez. He owes me a favour.'

'Why? What happened?' But Birdie's curiosity wasn't satisfied. The Deacon sighed and closed his eyes in exhausted sleep. Birdie busied herself in checking out her herbs, which were very few, while the wagon lurched on driven by Marco. After a while, bored and with nothing to do, she settled herself at the front of the wagon beside

Marco. She smiled at him. He hard-eyed her, his mouth a thin trap.

'Hello, I'm Birdie. Who are you?'

'I'm Marco, Rodriguez' elder son, and I've got a woman of my own so don't go making cow's eyes at me!'

'Huh! As if I should. I'm particular, I am,' she flounced, tossing her head. Then she gave him a sly sideways glance. 'You happy with your woman? She's good in bed, eh? You're a lucky man.'

He scowled. 'Whether she is or she isn't, isn't any business of yours. Rosa's a good mother...'

'Ah ... I get it. A better mother than lover!' She grinned. 'Don't you fancy a change?' She put out a tentative finger and stroked the side of his head and then tweaked his sideburns.

He reached up and slapped her hard across the face and she nearly fell out on to the dirt below and only saved herself by some quick clawing at the woodwork.

'You can save yourself the effort.' The

Deacon's bored voice came from behind. 'The Rodriguez family set much store by family life. It's the only good thing that old man Rodriguez taught his kids.'

Marco twisted and faced the man lying on the bed, the reins slack, the mules moving slowly now.

'You know my old man, señor?'

'Yes, we rode together many years ago. I once saved him from hanging. Ask any of his riders about the time the hell-fire preacher came along and shot the rope he was hanging by. I think he broke a leg in his fall. You see, the settlers had strung him up high, but he got away.'

'Si ... si ... I was there. I was but a child. I remember the man with the fiery eyes, all dressed in black, mouthing off about vengeance being the Lord's. Was that you?'

'It was.'

'Then you're a friend.'

'I am, so what are you going to do about it? What about that slimy little bastard out there?'

'Domingo? I should kill him, but he has much influence and the men who work for us, work for him also. He is using our spread as a homing ground for what he and the others do. The padre is old and infirm and still trusts Domingo and takes no mind of my brother and myself. Domingo has poisoned his heart against us. We are as nothing...' The anger in him came out like bitter poison, festering, twisting his guts.

'So? You have given me much to think about.' And again, The Deacon closed his eyes but this time Birdie wasn't sure whether he slept or not or whether he had some plan in his mind.

Clegg leaned over the emaciated figure of Rodriguez, conscious of the silent watchers outside the ramshackle cabin. Marco and Pietro lounged beside the door, watching, silent and suspicious for a wrong move. Birdie stood at the other side of the make-shift bed, nose wrinkling from the smell of the dying man. For there was no doubt

71

about it, Rodriguez had not long to live. Clegg stepped back. Even he was choked by the stench and he had faced some skin-crawling sights in his time.

'How long has he been like this?'

The two men looked at each other. Pietro, the younger son, answered. 'Ten ... twelve days perhaps longer. We had been out on the range for five days rounding up strays. The women said the old man was restless, wanted to ride out. They tried to stop him for he had been weak and suffering effects of fever for some time. He took off early one morning on an old lame grey. He was away all day and then he came riding in, lying across the back of the animal. He had been shot through the back.'

'So I see. Any ideas who did it?'

Marco stirred uneasily. 'He knows but will not say. We ask and he turns his head to the wall. Oh, he knows all right.'

'I don't think there is anything we can do.' Clegg looked at Birdie who silently shook her head.

'You've got to do something!' Now Marco strode across and looked down at the old man. 'Can you awaken him? Can you find out...?'

There was something in the tone of the voice. Clegg frowned.

'What's eating you, Marco? It's more than just your old father dying, isn't it?'

Pietro snapped words at Marco and then looked at Clegg suspiciously. If things didn't work out, the danger would come from Pietro. Clegg lifted his hands in a peaceful gesture.

'Look, hombres, I'm not wanting to pry. I'm sorry about your old man, but really I couldn't give a shit...'

Pietro scowled. Marco had the nearest thing to indecision on his hard face.

'Can you do something for him?'

Clegg looked at Birdie. 'What have you got in that bag of yours? Maybe we could ease him a mite.'

He was willing to promise anything to play for time. He had a gut feeling about this. As

73

long as they were trying to do something, they would be unharmed. If things went wrong, he sensed the smouldering suspicion and anger that surrounded them, would finally explode and then there was no saying what would happen. They would have as much chance of getting away as finding a virgin out there amongst the tattiest set of women he'd had the bad luck to come across. He controlled his desire to spit.

He watched Birdie rummage in her leather pouch. He hoped she was thinking on the same lines as he was. She was young, but she caught on fast. He held his breath. She looked up and smiled and held up a small package done up in a huge dried leaf.

'I think this might help.' She looked around the dismal room and at the lack of facilities. 'Can we have some boiling water?'

Pietro shrugged and Marco said doubtfully, 'I'll get my woman. She'll get what you want,' and he slouched out. A few moments later, a slatternly young woman with her blouse undone at the neck and a screaming baby just interrupted from its feed, came in with some reluctance.

She listened quietly while Birdie told her what was required. She nodded without speaking and went away. It was some time before she returned with a tin bowl and a black iron pan steaming and slopping water. She had evidently given the child to some-one and buttoned up her blouse. She looked to be no more than seventeen.

She then stayed to watch with large velvety brown eyes while Birdie, with Clegg's help, examined the old man and then turned him over to peer at the huge wound in his back.

Clegg shook his head but Birdie persisted. There were the first signs of gangrene from which came the sweet cloying stench. The bullet must have penetrated a lung and was lodged somewhere inside. Lead poisoning was already coursing around the old man's body.

Birdie worked fast while Clegg held him comfortably. The probing fingers made the old man groan and once his eyes fluttered as if he was aware that something was happening to him. Clegg bent low over him, hoping for a few words.

'Señor Rodriguez, who did this to you?' For a moment the old eyes opened wide and then drooped. Clegg cursed to himself. That information might have bought them their freedom.

The wound cleaned, Birdie took it on herself to clean up the dirt-encrusted body. He had fleas and she found herself scratching and the tirade to which she subjected Marco's woman was something to listen to and admire. Clegg smiled.

'You sure can use words. Where the hell did you learn all that stuff?'

Birdie grinned. 'Drovers aren't all big and silent with only one thing on their minds! You'd be surprised at what they tell you and the opinions they have about their pards!'

'Huh! Anyone ever discussed me with you?'

'What? About the most ruthless bounty-hunter whom they call *the* Clegg? Sure.

76

You're known as a double-shot, cougar-mean bastard who's not given to any god-damn pisswillying around and who's got ice in his veins and–' and now she laughed– 'and a good standing prick in his pants when he happens to use it!'

'You made that last bit up! You're a lying little bitch!'

'Not about the state of it. I only speak as I find.'

'I mean about the fellers talking about it.'

'Oh,' she answered innocently. 'It wasn't only the fellers who talk about you. You seem to have a reputation with the girls!'

'Oh! Oh, well...' And he shrugged and gave a grin. 'I think you'd better get on and save this old goat's life. You realize our lives might depend on it?'

She nodded, all teasing laughter drained from her face. She glanced at the waiting girl.

'Go, prepare soup for him to drink.'

'He can't drink.' The girl looked sulky. 'The old women tried.' She shook her head.

'Make thin soup. We soak cloth and trickle it on to his lips. Now go!' The girl was glad to go. Then Birdie looked up at Clegg.

'Mr Westerley knew Rodriguez many years ago. He owes him a favour.'

'Who? Westerley does or Rodriguez?' He ignored the usual feeling of anger the "mister" aroused. This was important.

'Rodriguez owes Westerley. Seems Mr Westerley saved his life.' Clegg clapped his thigh.

'By God! The best bit of news I've heard today. You know the Mex pride in honouring their obligations unto the fourth generation?'

'Yes, I know.' And now Birdie held her own head up with pride. 'I have Mex blood too. Honour can be a hard taskmaster if not carried out.'

'Does anyone else know?'

'Yes, Marco. He was surprised and impressed. It means we have to bring the old one around so that he recognizes Mr Westerley and then the obligation will fall on

Marco and Pietro.'

'Huh!' grunted Clegg. 'I wish there had been some other way. It means I'll be under obligation to The Deacon too, and *that* is something too hard to swallow!'

Birdie looked at him with astonishment.

'Goddammit, you sonofabitch! Would you rather we all die than take advantage of Mr Westerley?' Clegg's shoulders heaved expressively. 'I've got my pride too, Birdie Firehorse!'

The old man was sleeping. Twice his eyes had fluttered open and his throat had worked as if he was trying to say something. He had taken a little soup, clumsily administered by Rodriguez' woman. Now he was sleeping and Clegg and Birdie were taking advantage of going to their own wagon which was situated in front of the tumbledown ranch-house.

At one side of it was a badly-fenced corral and on the other a row of lean-to sheds which housed the miserable families who worked for Rodriguez. Clegg could see at a glance that the men were of the cut-throat variety, probably recruited by Domingo. It must have been a long time since Rodriguez was boss of his own spread.

Clegg knew the score. He'd seen it happen many times. A lax and boozy boss and a scheming segundo who gradually took over and fired and then hired his own men...

He thought of the two sons. Both blind to the situation. Probably been too young when the rot had set in and were tolerated only because they went along with what Domingo wanted to do. Clegg spat.

It was clear what must have happened. The old man's legitimate enterprise was now getting in the way of Domingo's ambitions. The old boss had to go. So Domingo or one of his men had shot the old man in the back, and the tough old nut had refused to die.

It was time Marco and Pietro understood the danger they were in too!

Back in the wagon, Clegg surveyed his

prisoner. The Deacon was looking perkier. Indeed, he had a slightly mocking smile on his face.

'You're looking better, Westerley. That muck Birdie's plastered you with must be great stuff. How's the leg?'

'I'll live, even though you tried to burn me to the bone. You're sure a rotten brander of beeves!'

Clegg's answering smile was wry. 'I never had to brand a calf in your condition. That rotten meat of yours took some frying, let me tell you. You're lucky to be alive.'

'Yeh, well, don't rub it in. You did it for your own sake, not mine!'

'Glad you realize that!' They glared at each other.

Birdie sighed. 'For God's sake! Stop chivvying each other. There's more serious things to talk about. What do we do, if those folk out there turn rough?'

'The usual. Shoot our way out. What else?'

Birdie shook her head in disbelief. 'What? With a wagon and four unhitched mules?

Don't make me laugh!'

'Don't fret about it. We'll keep that old man alive long enough to convince those sons of his that we did all that was possible. It's Domingo we want. Once convince the rest that it was Domingo who shot the old man the rest will be easy.'

'How do you figure that?' The Deacon was looking interested. He lay flexing his fingers which was a good sign.

'Any fool can figure who was behind the shooting. Domingo wants the whole caboodle. He's got the boys in a spot. They've been relying on him for years to run the place. They're nothing but a pair of loafers. They haven't even figured that they're next in line for the bullet.'

The Deacon's chin was sunk on to his chest. He glanced at Birdie.

'Did she tell you about Rodriguez and me?'

'Yeh, she mentioned it.' Clegg was being too casual.

'I think it's time I had a word in the old

man's ear. I know just the word to bring him back alive!'

'Oh? And what's that?'

The Deacon smiled slyly. 'If I told you, you'd know as much as myself.'

Clegg spat disgustedly, oblivious to where the glob landed. There was a faraway look on The Deacon's face as if something had just occurred to him. He turned and grinned at Clegg. 'By damn, it just might do it!'

Clegg fumed. He was damned if he was going to ask. But he was uneasy. The Deacon was suddenly confident. He wasn't just a prisoner with a gammy leg any more. He had something yeasting away in his mind, and by the look of him, Clegg wasn't going to like it very much.

Clegg made up his mind. They were getting out of this mountain range and away from this half-wild bunch at the first opportunity. And by God, he would make his own opportunity!

Four

'Don't just stand there! Help me up and take me across to see Rodriguez!'

Clegg stared at The Deacon, his mind going through all the possibilities. What in hell was this half-dead bastard cooking up now?

'Not in your state. You can't even stand on that bloody leg. Do you want to lose it altogether?'

'Don't be a fool. I've got over worse than this. Didn't you see the hole in my back?'

Clegg had to admit the scarred remains of a bushwhack wound had been impressive, as also had been the scars above his heart and ribs. The self-styled deacon who raved about hell and damnation when he was drunk certainly must have protection from that feller in the sky. That or he was just the luckiest man alive. However he raised his hands in protest.

'Do what you like as long as you don't rob me of what you're worth way back in Fort Smith!'

The Deacon's expression changed to that of a wolf.

'Blast your hide, Clegg, I'm doing this for you and the girl as well as myself. Play it right, feller, or I might just leave you both behind and light out by myself. I'm not fussy, y'know and I'm no gent when it comes to considering females. I would just as soon drop her into the shit as yourself. Make no mistake about that!'

'You're just the slime-bellied bastard I always thought you were. But let me tell you something, buster, no prisoner ever gets away from me. I aim to take you back, and that's all there is to it!'

Again they eyeballed each other. Two strong self-willed gunmen, both used to coming out on top. The Deacon looked down at his gammy leg. He could move it easier than he pretended. He owed Clegg for saving it and it irked him that he was in his debt. If he could get them all away from this cut-throat gang, then he would consider the debt paid. He would worry about outwitting Clegg at a later date. There was no way he was going to be led into Fort Smith bound like a parcel of piece goods.

'Get me up, Clegg, and stop your belly-aching. If we get out, we get out together. Now come on, hunker me up!'

Clegg was pulling him erect when Birdie entered the wagon. She looked from one to the other and was concerned for The Deacon's drawn white face.

'Stop bullying him, Clegg. What the hell do you think you're doing?'

'Aw, shut up, you little bitch! You've got a mouth like a bloody rattler's. He wants to be up to go a-visiting, that's what. I'm not always wanting to torment him, bastard as he is. So watch your mouth or else...'

'Else, what, Clegg?'

'One of these days I'm gonna paddle your

arse so that you won't sit down for a week. Believe me, I'm a mite heavy-handed.'

Suddenly she grinned and it confused him. Women! They were queer critters.

'What's so funny?'

'Nothing. Just a thought. Now if you were a bit nicer to me … like say, make sure I'm warm of nights, I might even wash my mouth out with carbolic!'

'Huh! Once a whore always a whore!'

Birdie's eyes flashed. 'There was a time when you begged me! What the hell's the matter with me now? Or is it that you don't like it free for fear I want to be your regular woman? You'd rather pay, go bang-bang and thank you ma'am and ride away knowing your bloody money would help keep me alive for another week! Is that it?' Her voice rose, and The Deacon, who was teetering on one leg, sighed deeply.

'Look, can't you keep your domestic quarrels to some other time? I want to see Rodriguez before my legs give out. For God or the devil's sake, Clegg, slap her down and let's get on with it.'

Clegg looked at Birdie and there was something more in his eyes than just exasperation. Something that made Birdie's mouth stretch with malicious amusement. Clegg wasn't just a cold killer who had everything under control all the time. It had been a long time since they'd lain together. His blood would be beginning to course despite himself. He wasn't *quite* in full control.

'I'll deal with you later. Now get out of the way and let me get this wayward fool off the wagon and over to the cabin. By the looks of his bandage, you're going to have to dress that wound again when I haul him back!'

Birdie watched them go, eyes unusually soft and mouth smiling.

From the shadow of the barn, Pietro watched. Birdie had sure made an impression on him. Instinctively he knew by the way she moved her hips and thrust out her bosom that she was what she was. He licked his lips. He'd often envied Marco sleeping every night with his woman, and she was no looker like this one was. He'd made up his mind that he was going to have her ... permanent, no matter what arrangement was made for the two gunmen. It was time he had a woman of his own. He moved up close behind her before she realized he was near. It was his smell that betrayed him. She turned swiftly to see the idiot-like smile as his eyes fastened on the exposed chest. She knew what was going on in his mind as well as down below.

'What do *you* want?' Her tone was sharp.

'You. What about coming into the barn? I'll pay you.' His fingers caught her upper arm and he squeezed her softness. She shrugged herself free.

'I'm not doing the business. I don't want your money.'

'But you're anybody's, aren't you? You should be lucky I'm willing to pay. I could take you without paying. Maybe you like a bit of the rough stuff? Makes it more exciting.'

She backed away. He followed. Her eyes

darted from side to side. Clegg and The Deacon had gone inside the cabin. If Pietro was to pounce and cover her mouth, it could be all over, by the state of him, before Clegg could know something was wrong.

Suddenly she lunged to the side. He followed and she kicked out with one leg in a movement she'd perfected years before. The familiar crunch as her foot went home made her smile and he to double up.

He screamed and dropped to the ground, rolling over and over, holding himself. She watched. There was no mercy in her. She never pulled her punches. But his fighting spirit was unquenched. Pietro might not know or understand women but he knew how to fight and ignore his own pain. He came up off the ground and grabbed her ankle and she found herself under him. Blind rage made him go for her throat. They rolled and she gagged and pummelled his back while the world went black and the strength went from her fists.

Suddenly there was the sound of a gunshot. The slug bit the dust beside Birdie's head and must have missed Pietro by a whisker. He whirled away from her, clawing for his gun. He was on his knees when Clegg said softly, 'It's a good thing I'm no bushwhacker. I could have got you plumb clean in the back. Now just get to your feet any way you like and we'll finish this now.'

Birdie lay on the ground, breasts heaving. There was a cut on her cheek, and her blouse was in shreds. It was plain to see what had been happening. She wanted to be sick. Clegg ignored her. He was watching Pietro, who was now standing in the well-known crouch with right foot forward. He was flexing his gunhand, hesitating, his red bandanna flapping under his chin. He'd lost his hat and his shock of badly cut greasy hair fell over his eyes. Sweat poured down his forehead and into his eyes, stinging and blinding. He licked his lips, now from fear and not from lust. He'd forgotten Birdie and what he wanted to do to her. His bowels were becoming loose. He had a gut pain...

Desperately he looked into the cold deadly eyes of Clegg who was standing ramrod straight with legs apart and both hands poised above his guns. He was out-gunned. He knew both those guns would spit fire if he moved. He only had one gun. Clegg's fingers flickered as if impatient to grab the well-worn grips. Pietro knew that both guns would come out of their covering holsters smooth and clean and deadly.

He swallowed. Then he saw Clegg's eyes move. They turned to Birdie.

'Move!' The word was like the crack of a whip. Birdie rolled away and Pietro went for his gun. He never knew whether it had ever come out of leather. All he knew was that his known world had exploded; his eyes opened wide as he felt a buffalo-kick blow to his chest which flung him high in the air. He was quite dead when he hit the ground.

Suddenly the area before the cabin was filled with women and children and those men chosen to guard the ranch. Clegg stood his ground, legs apart and guns smoking.

Behind him was the cabin.

There were shouts and screams and much jostling to see what was to see. No one felt inclined to challenge the gunman. Clegg was too fierce a figure for ordinary small-time rustlers to challenge.

'Where's Domingo?' Clegg roared. 'Rodriguez is awake and wants Domingo. Find him.' He ignored the body and those who stood sullenly watching. To Birdie, he said softly, 'You all right? Did he hurt you?'

She was sitting with her knees hunched up under her chin. She still felt dizzy and there would be some first-class bruises on her body tomorrow. She nodded, not given to whining. She'd been brought up tough.

'I'll live,' she muttered. 'Thank you for what you did. I think he would have strangled me. Sometime I'm going to thank you...' She smiled briefly and he shrugged.

'I might just hold you to that when all this is over.' Suddenly his attention was drawn to the little fat man coming from way past the corral. 'Get yourself to the wagon, Birdie,

and if you can, get those mules harnessed.'
She raised her eyebrows.

'Are we going somewhere?'

'You bet we are. I don't know what The
Deacon whispered into that old man's ear
but it sure woke up the old devil and he was
grinning up at Westerley like he was some
long-lost son. Wants to see Domingo pronto.'

Moodily he watched Domingo come
nearer, a young boy at his elbow. Domingo's
eyes were on Pietro's body. There was no
anger there. Instead, Clegg could have sworn
there was satisfaction.

Domingo paused beside the body and
toed it and raised his eyes to Clegg.

'I understand from the boy, you did it?'

'Yeh. He asked for it. Anybody can tell
you.'

Domingo nodded. 'It figures. He was
woman crazy. What's the old man want? I
understand he's back with us.'

'Yeh, come round fast when The Deacon
whispered in his ear. Know what it's about?'

Domingo gave his fat smile. 'Maybe,

maybe not. I'd better go and find out.'

He disappeared inside the cabin and Clegg slowly followed, scratching his bristly chin. He was just in time to hear The Deacon saying very positively, 'Yeh, old Rodriguez and I rode with Mossman twenty years ago. Mossman got out of the pen last year and I won the map in a crap game. Mossman died of unnatural causes a week afterwards.' He smiled and that smile wasn't good to see. 'I needn't go into details about it, only to say that Mossman changed his mind and wanted the map back. He told me you had one quarter of that map. So, how about it?'

Rodriguez lay shaking on his bed. He might have had the ague by the look of him but it wasn't that. It was the thought that someone close by had the rest of the map he'd guarded for so long.

He looked at Clegg standing just inside the door.

'What was with the shooting?' Clegg shrugged and moved his long lean length.

'Your son, Pietro was having woman

trouble.' The old hands clawed at the blanket over him.

'Your woman?'

'You might say that.'

'He was a fool! He kept his brains between his legs! So now there's only Marco and his children.' He sighed. 'So be it. Maybe it's for the best.'

Domingo, who had been silent, now frowned.

'Don't forget your segundo, old man. I've been like a loyal son to you.'

'You've made your pile, Domingo. I've known your little game. I'm no fool. A few beeves here, and a few beeves there and gradually your handpicked men taking over from mine. But it didn't matter, boy. I've always known I had an ace up my sleeve. There's more to life than a run-down ranch on the bleak edge of nowhere.'

Domingo flushed with anger.

'You were using me knowing you held a secret to riches?'

'Huh, why not! Even Marco and Pietro

didn't know about the piece of map.'

'And what if you'd died and it was never found?'

'I'd be in no position to worry, would I?' He grinned showing gapped yellow teeth, in a deathshead skull.

Clegg felt it was time to intervene.

'What the hell are you guys talking about?'

The Deacon grinned. 'Now why should we tell you? You, who wants to take me back to Judge Parker and either a hanging or a stretch in the pen? Now what makes you think I'm softhearted enough to tell you?'

Clegg set his teeth. 'The only reason I can think of is the fact that if you don't tell me, you'll never get the chance to use this map you set such store by. That's all!'

The Deacon laughed. 'And just what makes you think you'll live long enough to move that wagon of yours just one yard along the trail?'

'This!' And suddenly The Deacon was twisted around despite his wound and was standing with one arm thrust up his back and a gun pressing under one ear. 'Now how do you like your eggs boiled?'

The old man on the bed screwed up his eyes, taking in the situation.

'It appears you fellers don't like each other. A pity for there's enough silver stashed away to make us all rich.'

The Deacon felt the pressure ease on his neck.

'How about it, Clegg? I would rather you didn't know but as the old man's shot his mouth, you're in if you want in. What about it?'

'You're my prisoner and I'm taking you back. You're worth ten thousand...'

'Aw, shit! Your share of the silver would be ten times that! It's sitting there, waiting to be picked up. Mossman's last big screw-up. Got the silver bullion away from the Mexican soldiers, hid it in an old disused mine and then blew up the opening. Trouble was, he blew up nearly everyone else as well. Done it deliberate, I guess. But the soldiers were wily. Only half the detail went with the bullion. The rest caught up with Mossman and he got twenty years.'

'And where do you come in?'

'I was a kid. I hid in a hole for three days. Nearly died of thirst. What the hell else would I be doing down beyond Abilene when you caught up with me? I was on my way south and doing a job for Ben Sayle and the Pinscher outfit he runs with. Ben knew Mossman. They met in the pen. I remembered the mystery of the lost silver. I was on its track when I bumped into Mossman again. A bit of luck I needed. There was the matter of the Neuman girl. I'm not much gone on kidnap and drugging, but...' he shrugged. 'I was down on my luck. I needed the money to get me down to Mexico.'

'And I spoilt your little game and we're now going the wrong way.' Clegg was mocking. 'I find it a real pleasure to know that I'm bucking you, buster. If you live long enough it will be mighty fine to think of what old man Rodriguez is ferreting around for and you banged-up for the next twenty years!'

Clegg was being quite carried away with the idea of The Deacon being frustrated and in a torment of failure and so he forgot Domingo. Suddenly Clegg's triumphant grin changed to a grimace of pain as a gun barrel crashed down on the back of his head. His legs turned to jelly while his head exploded into a cluster of stars and he fell like an axed steer.

The Deacon looked down at him dispassionately. 'A pity. He would be a good man on our side.'

'What should I do with him?' Domingo looked up at The Deacon as to a new leader. 'Do you want him killed? He's asked for it.'

The Deacon shook his head. 'No, if anyone is going to kill him it will be me. I owe him that. Tie him up and sling him in the wagon.'

'What about you?'

'I think I might just be able to sit up and do a bit of driving.' He grinned. 'I'm a bit like this here old goat. I recover mighty fast!'

Birdie was shocked when Clegg was flung

like a side of beef into the wagon. The Deacon was there, being helped along by Domingo. His steely eyes caught and held hers.

'If I catch you undoing his knots, I'll flay the skin off your back!'

Birdie did not answer. The tone of voice didn't leave any doubts that he meant what he said. Again it occurred to her that Clegg might have been right. Mr Westerley was a man to watch, and maybe womanly wiles wouldn't have any effect on him. Now she only nodded.

Later, she put arnica on the egg-like bump. Clegg was going to have a king-size headache when he recovered. Inwardly she raged at The Deacon's treachery, for there was no doubt about it, he must have watched Domingo creep up behind Clegg. He'd given no warning, and Clegg had saved his leg! What bloody ingratitude!

Rodriguez was lifted into another ramshackle flat-bedded vehicle and though he looked as if he would expire with his next breath, his old eyes burned with a feverish gleam. Marco knelt beside him, taking the scrawny hand in his.

'Padre, is this a good thing? You are not strong enough to travel. How far do we have to go?'

The old man's eyes travelled past Marco to Domingo who was hovering close by.

'There are many flapping ears, chico. I want to be sure you and los niños get your share of the silver.' His chest heaved. 'I shall live long enough to see it so.' Then the rheumy old eyes took on a sly look. 'Remember, if anything should happen, the hombre called The Deacon is your friend.'

'What about Domingo?' Marco's mouth was against the old man's ear. Domingo scowled. He could not hear what was being said for the noise of dogs barking and the wails and calls from those who were going to be left behind.

The old man gave a long sigh. 'He was like a son to me, just as you are. Nay, I did wrong. I thought he was more loyal to me than you and your brother. But he went against my wishes. I could see what was happening but you chicos were too young to be strong against him. He has had all he will get from me. From now, all shall be yours.'

Marco's eyes gleamed. 'Padre, would it not be best if I...' A clawlike hand gripped Marco's wrist tight.

'No ... no! If you are going to say, kill him, I say no! Domingo was as a son to me until his head grew big with the power in him. It would bring bad luck to kill. Leave him. Maybe The Deacon will dispose of him!' A fierce amusement shook him until he coughed and hawked until his old chest threatened to give up the struggle to expand. His breath came raspingly. Marco was alarmed.

'Would it not be best if you gave me your piece of the map?'

'If the map was found on you, chico, then both of us might die! It is in a safe place, so don't worry.'

'But if you should die...'

'Don't worry! I shall not die until the right time.'

'But you must share the secret! This is ridiculous. I should know!'

'Then you will make sure I stay alive, eh, chico?'

Marco stepped back. 'You don't trust me either?' His mind worked furiously. He never thought to hear his father express doubts as to his loyalty. Anger tightened his voice. 'Maybe you should pay the other gun-man to watch The Deacon. They are already enemies, or better still cut him in and he will watch Domingo too. He will keep you alive!'

'Don't be a fool, chico. You know I want you to have the silver. Think, chico. Use your brains! If either of them tortured you and you knew where the map was, you're not strong enough to hold out.'

'How do you know? You have always treated me and Pietro as boys. We were never given responsibilities!'

'Because I didn't want you growing up as rustlers! I wanted a legitimate spread for you both. I didn't want you getting used to easy money and maybe finishing up hanging from a gallows tree!'

'Very well. We leave it as it is and if anything happens to you, then we kiss the silver goodbye!'

Rodriguez shook his head tiredly. 'The Deacon will look after you.'

'Mother of God! Do you really trust him?'

'As much as any man. After all, he is now under an obligation. We persuaded Clegg to let him go down to Mexico.'

'You call that persuasion cold-cocking him and tying him up? When he gets over the crack he'll be madder than a frustrated buffalo!'

'We'll see. He's got time to think about the silver bullion. He's a man who thinks a lot about big bucks. You'll see, he'll change his mind. It will be interesting seeing two giants pitting their wits against each other.'

'You're enjoying this, aren't you?'

'As much as a burnt-out hombre can enjoy anything. Better than lying on that stinking pallet and wondering whether I shall see another dawn.' Marco nodded slowly.

'You get all the rest you can, padre, and I'll go see what's holding everyone up.'

Outside the wagon, Paulo, Marco's nineteen-year-old son was waiting. He lounged against the back of the wagon waiting. He was detailed to drive and look after his grandfather.

'What goes on? Why aren't we ready to move out?'

Paulo grinned. 'Domingo is having a hard time with his woman. She says he will not come back and what will become of her.'

'Huh, typically woman-like. How is your stepmother taking it?'

Paulo looked at him curiously. He'd always known his father ducked out of responsibility if he could. He'd heard his grandfather call him weak to Domingo whom he feared. There was a little contempt in the twist of his lips.

'She doesn't want you back. As soon as she has her baby she will go to her own people and take the others with her.'

'Stupid woman! Always was headstrong. It is a pity your mother died.'

'You gave her too many dead babies.' There was something in Paulo's tone that made his father stare hard at him. A thought went through his mind that soon Paulo would be a man and a strong-minded one at that. Maybe he would take watching...

He scowled. 'I'll go and talk to her myself.'

When he was gone, Paulo climbed inside the wagon to his grandfather's side.

'Do you want anything, grandfather?'

The old man shook his head but reached out for his hand.

'You're a good boy, Paulo. I trust you and you have a close mouth. Now listen carefully to what I have to say...'

Paulo's eyes gleamed. He nodded.

'I understand, grandfather. The map is hidden in the...'

Rodriguez raised a trembling hand. 'Don't say it, chico, don't even think it. Just remember!'

Clegg cursed as Birdie tended his bump. His head ached as if a cleaver had split it in two.

'Come on, we're friends, aren't we? Undo these knots.'

Birdie shook her head. 'I daren't. Mr Westerley sounded as if he meant what he said. I'm beginning to think you might be right about him. I'm sorry, Clegg. I'll help you the moment it's safe, honest I will.'

Clegg groaned. 'Well, just loosen them a bit and I'll work on them.'

'Really, I daren't, Clegg. Let's see if he comes to inspect them and maybe afterwards ...!'

'You're a windy critter,' he grumbled. 'What's it with a lame man? Surely you know I wouldn't let him hurt you.'

'Talk's cheap. Look at the state of your hands. You won't be able to scratch your arse with those for a few days when you get free.'

'If, you mean,' he muttered savagely.

'Anyone could stick a knife in me any time. I wonder why he hasn't done it?'

'Because he's a gunman like you and just as foolish. He would rather face you and give you a chance and prove once again he's the best! I don't know why you ask. You're just the bloody same.'

There was a shout outside, and Birdie poked her head out of the wagon. Some of Domingo's boys were hauling The Deacon on to the wagon. He gave Birdie a penetrating glance. She shivered. He would have known instantly if she'd disobeyed him.

'Everything all right in there?'

She tried to lie. 'Yes, he's ... er ... still out.'

'Is he now? I didn't think his head would be that soft. Maybe I should look.'

'No! He's all right. Just leave him. He's got a helluva lump on his head.'

The Deacon smiled. 'Done your doctoring, eh? Well, tell him he can take over the driving when his head decides to become part of him again.'

'What does that mean, buster?' Clegg's

voice came from behind them.

'Oh, so you're back from the dead? The little lady doesn't quite tell the truth. I'll remember that.' He beamed at Birdie. She felt her heart start pounding. She'd thought Clegg cold and calculating, but this man was like one dead without feeling or nerve or compassion. How had she been such a fool as to think him her father's friend and now hers? The long-drawn-out memories of him had been wishful thinking and she'd built on them herself because she'd been alone in the world. She turned away from him, to hide her eyes that might betray her. She still had her woman's guile.

At last the cavalcade moved forward. Domingo's four outriders flanked the wagons. Four extra horses were tethered, two behind each wagon and Domingo headed down the mountain the same way as they'd come. But down below they left the main trail and hit an old Indian track and bumping and lurching, the wagons inched slowly forward. Their new destination was roughly a hundred miles beyond the Rio Grande or so The Deacon had assured Domingo. He was trusting the Mexican to lead them across country in the shortest time possible.

'And what of the big man? What do you do with him?' Domingo had asked The Deacon with avid curiosity. Maybe The Deacon was good with a knife. The Deacon shrugged.

'What do two professional gunmen do? They settle it once and for all, who's the best man. One of us will die.'

Domingo looked at him incredulously.

'You will risk your life when you could slide a knife in his ribs right now?'

'We do things differently than you do, Domingo. Now if it was you...' He grinned into the fat face. 'You're a knife man and you aim for the back, therefore I should do the same. It would be a matter of wits. Comprendez?'

Domingo laughed easily. 'But the knife is my weapon. You would be at a disadvantage.'

'Yes?' Before Domingo could blink, The

Deacon's arm flashed up and over and he'd drawn a blade from just below his nape and it whirled and twinkled in the sunlight and thudded into one of the uprights of the leading wagon. It quivered there, heart high and Domingo looked at it with mesmeric fascination. He swallowed.

'I didn't know...'

'There's lots you don't know about me, amigo...'

Domingo pondered this as he rode ahead with two of his boys half a horse's length behind. He was taking no chances; he'd already got a plan thought out. It only meant filling in the details once the silver was located. There was no way he would share it with the weak and spoilt Marco and certainly not with The Deacon and he would make damn sure the man called Clegg was quietly slaughtered. Benissimo was the best man for the job. He could belly through grass like a snake. Then there was the boy Paulo ... he was young. He must think about him. He had no time for his father, maybe he would come in with him. The boy could be useful...

The days passed painfully slowly. It was gut-churning spine-cracking travelling; at least Birdie, straightening her back, found it so. She was thoroughly sick and tired of the whole idea of improving her condition. She wished bitterly she'd stayed back in Batuco where the pickings were small but usually plentiful and there had always been the hope that she might meet someone special. Her thoughts of Clegg were sour. She'd been sure that he would be the one ... he'd been so different from the usual punter. At least he'd bathed and shaved before coming looking for a woman.

But since The Deacon had allowed him to be freed, now that they were in the wild country he'd never come near her. When she taunted him he'd looked at her grimly and reminded her that there was no way he would share her blankets and leave his back vulnerable to attack, which was reasonable when you considered it. At least it wasn't that he didn't want her. She saw the look in his eyes.

That look had sparked off an interest from another quarter. To make life difficult for Clegg she'd made eyes at young Paulo. He was only a boy and it amused her to make him jump when she snapped her fingers. He was like a puppy learning new tricks, and then one night she learned something herself. He wasn't such a young pup after all…

Now her thoughts and the throbbing of her body made of him an obsession. After all, he was only a couple of years or so older than herself. He was all passion and hungry for more of what she'd offered him for free. She refused him and his frustration filled the boring dust-laden days. She tantalized him, promised with her eyes and then rejected him until even The Deacon intervened and the boy was sent ahead on horseback with Domingo while Marco drove his father's wagon.

'We're going to have trouble with that hot-arsed little bitch,' The Deacon confided in

Clegg. 'Why the hell don't you do something about it? She wants you, not that wet-
behind-the-ears kid. All this is for your
benefit. What's the matter with you? Getting
old?'

Clegg shrugged. There was a kind of un-
spoken armistice between them. Neither
spoke of what would happen when they
reached the cache of silver.

'I don't fancy getting speared like a fish in
a puddle just when things are getting
interesting. Haven't you noticed how our
friends watch her? Any damn one of them
would snuff out the first feller to bring a
groan out of her!'

'What about the kid? By the way he's been
huffing around, I think he's had a taste.'

'If he has, then he's lucky to be still
around. I think she's got more sense than to
have him again. Maybe one of us should
have a word with her and remind her she's
not got the shelter of the cat house.'

'You do it. You're the one who brought her
along.'

Clegg did so and got a lot of bullshit for his pains. She accused him of being dog-in-the-manger. He reminded her of Domingo and the others, but it was old Rodriguez who was still holding on grimly to life who finally convinced her. He wanted Paulo alive. He called Paulo into the wagon and when he clambered down later, he was hanging his head and after that he refused to catch Birdie's eye. It made her pig-sick.

So she was pleased when finally the day came when Rodriguez was propped up so that he could see the terrain and he tremblingly confirmed that they were on the right track to the place where the soldiers had been ambushed.

'Thank God for that,' The Deacon said fervently. 'Now we'll get set for marking off the spot before any other disaster happens.'

Crossing the Rio Grande had lost them two of Domingo's boys. Not that The Deacon worried much about that but it made them more vulnerable. He was beginning to worry about Clegg. The bastard was being too quiet.

The Deacon could now use his leg. Sometimes he rode one of the spare horses. He wouldn't admit that his leg ached and kept him awake nights: that was his own private affair. No need to give Clegg and Domingo ideas. Marco he dismissed as a nearly man, his boy had more spirit than he had.

Now he climbed into the old man's wagon.

'Well? What about that map? When do we see it?'

'I'll tell you when. We've another two days travel yet.'

'I hope you know what you're doing, old man. The next time I ask you, I want to see your part of it, or something drastic is going to happen. Right?'

The old man nodded and Clegg who was watching from the opening saw the sudden fear in the old man. It occurred to him that maybe The Deacon was wrong and that old Rodriguez had pulled a bit of the old bluff. Maybe he hadn't got the map from Mossman. Only knew about it and knew the vague location. Now that was a thought! But he kept the notion to himself.

Whatever happened at the end of this trek, he was going right back the way he came with The Deacon hamstrung to his horse, no matter what. It was just a matter of time...

That night over the campfire, Domingo aired his disquiet to Marco. On this trek, alliances had been made and broken and then re-established over and over again. Domingo had been shaken when two of his best men had been washed away in a flash flood in the raging tumbling waters of the river known as the Rio Grande. They had been lucky to get the wagons across before the unheralded waters burst about them. He was still shaken. If it hadn't been for the silver he would have turned back, his superstitious mind full of doubts and forebodings.

'What you say, Marco? Let's tackle the old man together. After all, you're his son. He's bound to tell you even if he won't tell me. We could ransack the wagon...'

Marco remained silent. He'd told no one about his father refusing to confide in him. The humiliation still burned deep. He stirred the fire with his boot and sparks flew.

'I've already searched the wagon. There's nothing but the food we carry, and the water barrel. There isn't space to hide a fish-hook never mind a map.'

'It must be on him then. Ask Paulo. He's the one who's been looking after him. He'd tell you if he'd seen it.'

Marco pursed his lips. 'I think Paulo would have told me before now if he'd seen it. I have warned him to look out for it. Told him it was very valuable and what could happen if it was lost. The boy hasn't seen it.'

Domingo raised his voice in temper. 'Then where the hell is it?'

'Maybe it isn't anywhere. Maybe it's in his head!' The two men looked at one another. Neither had thought of that possibility.

'The old devil...' Domingo began.

'By God, no wonder the old sonofabitch wouldn't...' Marco closed up sharp as

Domingo frowned.

'Wouldn't what.'

'Never you mind. It's no business of yours!'

'You mean you've already asked the old bastard and he wouldn't tell you? What kind of a father is he who doesn't tell his own son, for God's sake!'

'The kind of man who would put his segundo before his own sons and the segundo encouraged him!'

Suddenly Marco was challenging, a little rot-gut happy and furious. He wasn't going to take Domingo's contempt a minute longer. He fumbled for his gun and drew wildly as he sprang to his feet. He faced Domingo over the fire with the sparks still whirling upwards and did not see Domingo's hand flash or the whirr of steel as the knife embedded itself in his chest, his hand tightening in anguish as he catapulted backwards. The gun exploded but the bullet hummed harmlessly out into space. Domingo was retrieving his weapon when The

Deacon and Clegg appeared from the old man's wagon and the two remaining outlaws along with Paulo left their cards to gather round.

Birdie, looking out from the other wagon saw the grim faces, ducked again inside. It looked mighty like a showdown...

Five

There was a scuffle of movement behind Clegg. He turned in time to see old Rodriguez climb shakily off the makeshift bed. He caught him as he fell to his knees.

'Hold it, old man. You shouldn't be out of bed.' And he gently helped the old man to sit swaying, head hanging on his chest, on to the hard bed.

Rodriguez held up his head with an effort, his skull-like head awesome, his expression tragic.

'What is it? A fight over the cards or...' he swallowed, 'a showdown with Marco and Domingo?' His dead eyes pleaded with Clegg to give him the right answer.

Clegg hesitated, not because of sparing the old man's feelings but because he had the secret of the map. Telling an ill man that his son was knifed to death wouldn't do much for a frail heart. 'Well? What is it?' Suddenly all old Rodriguez' remaining strength was in the words he uttered.

'It's Marco. Domingo got the drop on him.'

'He used his knife? I was always afraid of that years ago.' The wasted body sagged. 'Two sons and both gone.' He raised his head again as if it weighed a ton and gazed at Clegg and two tears ran slowly down his cheeks. 'It's all my fault. I drove a wedge between them and Domingo. At one time I had great hopes for Domingo ... so vigorous, so loyal and full of ideas. It was only when I wanted to build up the ranch that the clash of loyalties came. He knew I wanted the ranch for my boys. He wanted it for himself, and I allowed myself to be blinded because my boys never really grew to be men! Now it is too late...'

'You have Paulo. You must think of him, and there are the other children. They need a better future than you yourself started out with. What about the map and the silver? I understand there is enough for all.'

Clegg thought that Rodriguez must have something on his mind. His expression changed at the mention of Paulo. Clegg had one of his gut feelings. Rodriguez looked positively smug.

'What is it, Rodriguez?' An incredible thought shot into his consciousness. Surely Rodriguez hadn't trusted Paulo when he wouldn't trust his own son? Casually he said softly, 'Paulo knows where the map is, doesn't he?'

Rodriguez reared up and the blood coursed in a dark purple blur across the pasty face. His breath came fast and gasping and Clegg thought, Christ! I've gone and done it now, the old devil is going to have a stroke!

'How did you know that?' The words came in a strangled dry whisper.

Clegg shrugged. 'You told me, or at least your eyes told me. I've just realized.'

'Then The Deacon and Domingo don't know?'

'Of course not. It's never occurred to them.'

'Will you promise to protect Paulo from Domingo? I know The Deacon will help you. Domingo would kill Paulo. He never had no time for the boy.'

'That figures. He was another who stood in his way. Yeh, I'll look out for Paulo.'

'And when the time comes and Paulo reveals the map, you'll be there with your guns at the ready?'

'If it comes to that, yes.'

'Good. Then I can die happy.'

'Yeh, well don't think of going yet!' The old man smiled and pulled down his lips.

'Why try to fight it? I'm quite ready.'

'Yeh, well...' Suddenly Clegg stopped abruptly. The old body had crumpled and the head appeared to roll from his shoulders. 'Hell!' Clegg ground out furiously. 'The bloody old devil's gone and let go!'

He gently laid the body down on the bed and on an unaccustomed impulse crossed the bony hands on the narrow chest. Then he stepped outside to a taut discussion going on between The Deacon and Domingo while Paulo watched white-faced and upset and the two remaining Mexicans watched with curious eyes, but not ready to intervene.

They were standing twenty feet apart. Domingo's knife was in his hand, and The Deacon stood in his usual crouch, but Clegg saw that he was favouring his wounded leg. The long flexible fingers moved slightly poised above his two Colts. Domingo's eyes were on them. Those hands alone held back Domingo who stood at bay like some animal. He licked plump and pouted lips.

'Señor, be reasonable. What is Marco to you? Why should you care that he got a knife in him? It was sure to be, sooner or later. Marco was a nothing man. He was no leader. He would never have controlled a crew or run a spread. He has been like a burr under a horse's saddle ever since he was born, along with that trashy brother of his.' There was cold contempt in his tone. He spat on the ground, watching those expressive hands.

The Deacon glanced sideways at Clegg. It was one of those moments when Clegg might have made an issue of who was boss in these parts. The Deacon felt a strange sense of brotherhood with this man. He was reluctant to admit it to himself, but the fact was that in other circumstances they could have been pards. He hated the idea but it was so. As it was, he appreciated Clegg standing back and letting him resolve this argument with Domingo. After all, Domingo was an enemy of both of them.

'Why so long? I expected you at my back.'

Clegg gave him an oblique smile. 'Now why should you think that? I'm still taking you in, Westerley.'

'Because the situation has changed. Were you just keeping out of trouble?' The thinly disguised mockery brought a heat to Clegg's cold face.

'No. The old man's dead.'

'The hell he is!' Clegg enjoyed the dismay on both men's faces. 'Great mince-meat balls! What do we do now?'

Domingo made a move and The Deacon's hand blurred and one Colt was aimed at the fat man's throat. Clegg watched interestedly. Now just how much faster was he than Westerley? Or wasn't he? It would be interesting to find out. But not yet. Domingo froze.

'What should we do with this jasper?'

'Tie him on his horse and throw away that damned butcher's knife!' Clegg's answer was terse and to the point.

'I think the little bastard should sweat first. He can dig a hole to bury Marco with old Rodriguez. Maybe the old man would like that.'

Clegg glanced at The Deacon. He never thought Westerley would have any sense of justice or sentiment of any kind. He warmed to him a little more. He grinned.

'Maybe it would be easier in the long run if we dropped him in the hole alongside them both after he dug the hole. What d'yer think?'

Domingo broke out in a sweat. He shook.

'*Madre mia!* I killed Marco. It was nothing to do with you,' he squeaked. 'Why kill me? As you say, there is enough silver for us all ... that is, if we can find Rodriguez' part of the map.' Suddenly he looked sly. 'Did he tell you before he died, señor?' Clegg shook his head, face inscrutable. 'Hell then! What do we do now?' Domingo screamed, forgetting the danger of the situation in his anger and frustration.

'You dig a hole and then we'll be on our way. After all, The Deacon here has part of the map.'

Domingo nodded. 'Then you will not kill me?'

'No. Maybe we will need all hands to haul the load. It depends how much was on that wagon train.'

Domingo nodded quickly and Clegg allowed him to approach the wagon. He took a long look at the body and then crossed himself.

'He was like a father to me,' he muttered to himself as he went and found the shovel strung up on the back of the wagon.

Four hours later, they were on their way, Birdie and Paulo driving one wagon and one of the Mexicans driving the other while Clegg and the Deacon forked horses. It was a damn sight better than picking up callouses on their arses. Domingo rode beside them, knifeless and his ankles tied to his horse. They left his hands free to guide his horse.

Then suddenly they were at the top of a long rolling valley. Far in the distance were three gigantic peaks that stood in a line.

'The Three Sisters,' breathed The Deacon with satisfaction. 'Down below, somewhere under the middle Sister is a deserted silver mine. That lost load was the last to be hauled out. Somewhere between here and those hills is the place where the massacre took place. Now if only we had the rest of the map...' There was anger in him. He had been quiet and moody since they resumed their journey after the burying. Clegg had been secretly enjoying the situation. Maybe the map would become a bargaining point. Suddenly Clegg realized that his earlier resolve to take The Deacon in was slipping. Ten thousand bucks against ... how much?

He sat back on the strong-backed gelding, comfortable in the thought that all his options were good ones.

There had been no opportunity to tackle Paulo on the journey. He and Birdie kept close together. He'd seen the look of strain on the youth's face. He was probably wondering when would be the right time to bring out the hidden map. Clegg smiled to himself. The kid would be pissing his britches and wondering whom to trust. He'd not confided in Birdie, that was clear, unless Birdie was playing some game of her own. A coldness had grown up between them. Clegg put it down to Paulo and his availability. Birdie didn't yearn after Clegg any more. A pity really, but things hadn't turned out as Clegg intended them in the first place. If it had been only The Deacon and Clegg and the girl travelling peacefully to Fort Smith, then a tied-up Deacon would have been no threat and he and Birdie could have indulged quite freely. As it was, he was too old for shenanigans under pressure.

Now he waited and wondered. It was time he and Paulo had a little talk. He wished he knew where the one-time prisoner had his part of the map stashed. It would have made life easier. He pictured The Deacon's face, if ever he could get the two parts of the map and join them together and then wave them under Westerley's nose … he grinned. That would be worth the inevitable shoot-out.

That night when they stopped to make camp and Domingo, tied to a prickly scrub bush, was eating his food, Clegg managed to follow Paulo when the boy wandered off into the bush to find a place to crap.

'Paulo, I must talk to you.' He ignored the poor boy's start as he crouched and did the business.

Paulo finished hastily and grabbed a tuft of grass and then yelped as a thorny bit scraped his arse.

'What do you want to talk about?' he said with tears in his eyes.

'About the map. It's time you handed it over, preferably to me.'

Paulo bit his lip. 'How do I know I can trust you?'

Clegg shrugged. 'You can't, but you haven't much choice. It's either me or Westerley and he doesn't know I know you have it. I do. Your grandfather told me,' he said, stretching the truth. 'He made me promise to look after you. Get your share and all that.'

'So he trusted you?'

'You might say that. What about it?'

'Well, I was worrying about what to do. I had this nightmare about telling someone and then getting my throat slit. I wouldn't like Domingo to have been the one to find out.'

'No, well he's out of it. You're lucky I'm here to help you.' Clegg's cold face relaxed and though the eyes did not warm up, there was something about him that made Paulo take heart.

'I don't want any trouble. I only want to get out alive and take Birdie away and maybe set up myself on the ranch. There's still the beeves and what with my share of the silver...' His voice trailed away.

'You could take care of your brothers and sisters and your step-mother and maybe marry Birdie?'

Paulo's face flushed. 'Yes, that's what I want. You will help?'

Clegg considered. He couldn't remember any youngster ever asking for his help before. This youth was innocent and vulnerable and he liked Birdie. He'd never had a close family. Strangers had always been targets with a price on their heads. Most folk had been wary of him. None had ever wanted his friendship. It had been a lonely independent life. He'd never wanted any other. He'd always enjoyed what he did. He got great satisfaction from trailing a man with a price on his head. They weren't men, they were lower than animals. If he'd taken

The Deacon in without trouble, he would have collected and gone on his way with never another thought as to the man's fate.

It was only in the long silences of the night he allowed himself to think of Molly and her family. He'd never before had wanted a wife until he'd seen that pretty innocent face, the blonde hair and the laughing blue eyes...

It was then that the iron control melted and white-hot fury against The Deacon erupted. It was then when Clegg was tempted to creep up on him and choke out his life. The bounty on him had saved his life, otherwise he would have been a dead man.

Now he considered Paulo. He was conscious that somehow he'd changed. Some iced-up place deep inside him was melting. His regard for The Deacon was subtly changing. The bastard had taken on character and form. He actually respected the bastard for his gun-toting abilities and as for this boy, he was willing to help him and the worst thing was, he was feeling a sneaking pleasure as if Paulo was his son and only he could help him. Jeeze! He must be going loco!

He found himself nodding.

'Yeh, I promised your old grandfather. I'll help you,' and the boy's relieved smile and the glow in his eyes made Clegg want to straighten his back, walk tall.

Clegg stared at The Deacon across the leaping flames of the fire.

'What about it, Westerley, when are you going to show me the map?'

The Deacon looked wary. 'Who says I'm going to show you it? We're gonna have a look round this valley first. Now if we'd had the old man's map it would have been simple. I think the old bastard had us conned.'

'Yeah? Well, I don't believe so.'

The Deacon frowned. 'What makes you say that?'

'Because I've got it here in my pocket.' Clegg's right hand hovered over his gun.

'The hell you have!' The Deacon made as if to draw and then was looking down the business end of Clegg's Colt.

'You sonofabitch!'

Clegg smiled. 'Yeh, and don't forget it. Now what do we do? We either call a truce for three days and look up each draw of this damn valley like civilized humans, or we fight it out right now. Winner buries the dead and looks after these folks and splits the silver when it's found. You choose. I'll just say one thing, I'll bury you deep so the coyotes don't dig you up!' His smile was mocking, confident.

The Deacon ground his teeth. 'I don't know how the hell you found the map and I'm not bloody interested, but I'm damned if I haul my body all this way with a gammy leg just to shoot it out with you, before we do any hauling. I want you to sweat first, see that raw silver, feel it, taste it and then know you'll never own any of it. I too can bury you deep when the time comes!'

'Well said. It's going to have to come to it,

doesn't it, Westerley? We've got to know, haven't we? One of us must be just a touch faster...'

'And that's me, buster!'

Clegg only smiled. They would find out before they left this godforsaken valley...

They sat brooding and staring into the fire, both enveloped in their own thoughts. Birdie and Paulo could be heard giggling in their wagon. It seemed that now Paulo's worries had been shared and he'd given up the map, he was much more uninhibited with Birdie, and she was loving it.

The Mexicans hunkered down near Domingo. They too had lit a fire. They sat well away from Domingo as a precautionary measure. They feared the two Americanos. Neither wanted to become an unnecessary target or be accused of releasing Domingo from his bonds. They passed a bottle around and gradually their voices rose as they relaxed. The Deacon viewed them morosely.

'I could do with a drink. You sonofabitch didn't give me a chance to bring a bottle

139

along.' He passed a dry tongue over his lips. 'Hell! I've nearly forgotten what it tastes like!'

Clegg got up without a word and went to the unoccupied wagon and came back and dropped a bottle at The Deacon's feet. He was remembering what Birdie had said about The Deacon when he was drunk. There was something he wanted to know, and he didn't intend asking when he was sober.

The Deacon stared up at him. 'What's this? An overture of friendship or that truce you were talking about?'

Clegg shrugged. 'Take it how you will. You wanted a drink. There it is.'

The Deacon stared at it. 'You haven't put something in it to give me the shits? There must be a catch!'

Clegg laughed. 'Oh, ye of little faith! Here, give it to me. I'll take first swig.' He took the bottle and pulled the cork and The Deacon's mouth worked as Clegg took a long slow drink. Then he sighed and rubbed the neck of the bottle. 'Here, you fool. I don't know why I bother. I'm giving good liquor to a bastard I hate!'

The Deacon drank, his hard eyes watchful. He couldn't quite make Clegg out. Bounty-hunters were usually impersonal, just doing a job. There was the business about the Coulsons. That had been bad. He'd been made to look all bad and that episode had been the girl's fault. He drank deeply. Yes, that girl had done something to Clegg. Made him vulnerable. Turned him from a hunting machine into something nearly human.

At the beginning he hadn't cared to put Clegg right about the rape and the subsequent killing of her family. He'd genuinely wanted to settle in Twofork Creek. But the girl, he would never forget how a nice innocent girl could ... he took another swallow. What the hell ... the sonofabitch should know there was more to her than just her blue eyes...

He held up the bottle. 'Want ... another...?' and found Clegg smiling at him as if he wanted The Deacon pissed. 'You wanna drink?'

Clegg shook his head. 'You drink it. I'm not in the mood.'

'You figuring to ask me about Molly?' The Deacon belched.

'Sort of.'

'Then I'll tell you.' Suddenly he found it difficult. He'd been a bastard in his lifetime but there had been one or two special women and he remembered being seared by a bitch way up in Wyoming that he'd figured on marrying. The cow had taken all his dough and gone off with a gambler. There'd been enough fury in him to kill two big-mouth fellers. A shot of caution made him take another drink. How would this big man take it?

'Well? Are you going to talk?' Clegg's eyes were glittering and his fingers drummed on his knees as he hunkered down by the fire. 'Why did you kill them all? They were good people.'

The Deacon took a deep breath. Suddenly

he didn't like the idea of telling Clegg what Molly was. Not from fear, but disgust at himself for wanting to enjoy this man's pain.

'Look, do you really want to know? It's done isn't it? You won't get them back.'

'God damn you! Of course I want to know!' Clegg beat the ground with his hammer fists. 'I could change my mind and take you back and the court would make you tell it as it was.'

The Deacon smiled. 'Ah ... so you were thinking of forgetting Fort Smith?'

'Yes, I was tempted. That silver sounds good, but by God, I think I was wrong!'

'Then you sonofabitch, here goes. She was no good, Clegg. She came after me with her baby blue eyes and her innocent pouting lips and her wish to learn more about the Lord's work and go out an' help those in need. She tempted and acted helpless ... she smiled and she coaxed...'

'You lying bastard! Molly wasn't like that!'

The Deacon was suddenly spreadeagled on his back, Clegg astride of him, hammering at his head. Taken by surprise, The Deacon writhed and ducked the blows, hampered by his still unhealed leg. He felt the pull of the puckered wound and set his teeth. He could feel the hot gush of newly-released blood. He steeled himself against the pain and grabbed and gouged at Clegg until he could give one mighty heave and catapult Clegg over his head. Then both men were up on their knees, clawing and grasping, Clegg's cold eyes lit up with a nearly mad glare.

'Hold it! Hold it!' The Deacon spat out the words as they feinted and closed with each other. 'I knew you wouldn't be able to take the truth!' he gasped as they slugged at each other with more strength than expertise.

'You bastard! I'll kill you slowly, inch by bloody inch...' The mad glare in Clegg's eyes did not diminish. It seemed to burn brighter at each savage blow. The Deacon's eyes were in danger of closing. There was a cut on his cheek and marks of steel-grip fingers at his neck. But Clegg hadn't got off freely. He too showed where The Deacon's defensive punches had struck home. Both men were gasping when suddenly Clegg's head exploded.

'What the hell...' He just registered surprise when the whole world went black. He fell on top of The Deacon who was trapped. He lay looking up at a grinning Domingo backed up by his two Mexican supporters. Three guns, and The Deacon recognized his own rifle amongst the three and he cursed as he lay helpless.

'You gave me just the chance I was looking for. Now it's my turn!' He glanced at the Mexicans who were now grinning at the turn of events. 'Fasten them both up and make the thongs tight. These bastards aren't to be trusted. Do it while the devil there is out. Now I'm going over to that other wagon. Seems to me they've been busy enough. It's my turn with the girl. You two can have her later!'

He strode across to the other wagon. It was

situated a little away from the other. Birdie had shown some delicacy. She'd insisted on being alone with Paulo. There was no need to rub Clegg's nose in the shit just because she'd found another man. It was the reason neither of them in the throes of excitement heard the fighting going on outside.

Now, she sat up on the makeshift bed, sheltering her bare breasts with crossed arms. Domingo pulled the canvas to one side and stood in the opening.

'Domingo! What the hell do you want? You're supposed to be tied up.'

Birdie felt Paulo tense up beside her. He lay partially covered by the shared blanket.

'First, I want Paulo. I want to know if his grandfather talked to him before he died, or gave him something. After that, I want you.' His smile was slow and deliberate as if anticipating a feast. He raised the shotgun he'd acquired.

Birdie looked down the twin muzzles and gulped and then the woman's wit returned.

'Use that and you'll not have either of us.

Where's Clegg and Mr Westerley?'

'You needn't worry about them. They're both tied up.' He grinned. 'As for the other, you needn't worry. I'll keep you as long as you're useful to us. As for that son of a spineless arse-licking daddy's boy, he can talk or be staked out on an anthill until he does! They say the ants are biting good this year. He can choose to talk, or else.'

'Why, you rotten slime-eating bastard...'

Domingo cocked the shotgun. 'Shut your face, bitch. I didn't say I wouldn't take a carefully placed potshot at you. I could pepper your legs or your back. You would still be of use, but slightly uncomfortable.' His lips pouted and tutted and then losing control he screamed at her, 'Hold that bloody tongue or I might cut it out!'

Then he was grabbing for Paulo's ankle. The boy was shivering but he kicked out and caught Domingo a boneshaker just under the throat. The fat man rolled and gagged and Paulo leapt out of the bed and grabbed up a wooden chest filled with flour and threw it at

Domingo. Unfortunately it missed and the lid flew open and flour poured everywhere and puffed up in clouds blinding them all. Domingo coughed and cursed as Paulo scooped up handfuls of flour and bombarded him with it. But finally Domingo got his fat arms about the boy's ribs and squeezed and Paulo squirmed and kicked but could not loosen the hold.

Birdie, coughing and wheezing, slipped out of the wagon to regain her breath. It was then she saw the whip they used on the mules. Grabbing it, she re-entered the wagon and though restricted, she laid about Domingo's shoulders and back.

He yelled and his hold on Paulo slackened and Paulo took advantage and turning swiftly kicked Domingo in the groin. He screamed and lost his balance and as he rolled near the opening, Birdie struck out with the whip and then lifted her own foot. Domingo hit the ground with a gut-shaking crack.

But it was too late. Clegg and The Deacon were securely fastened and the two Mexi-

cans closed in and Birdie was quickly over-
come although she bit and kicked until she
was knocked unconscious.

Paulo was another matter. He put up quite
a struggle doing much damage to Benissimo's face before the other Mexican was
free to help out. Then they trussed him up
like a turkey ready for the pot.

Meanwhile, Domingo was sitting up,
groaning. From him came a steady stream
of obscenity, between groans, aimed at
Birdie. She heard the threats with growing
fear. She'd handled this all wrong. She
should have used all her professional expertise, even to exploiting her body. Better a
soiled whore than a stiff! But now the
damage was done. Or was it?

Her brains started working again with the
desperation of one who knows all is lost and
nothing worse can happen. Things could
only get better. She smiled at the younger
Mexican, and he looked across at Benissimo
to see if that suggestive lifting of the lips and
the sweeping glance of dark eyes had been

noticed. He smiled back and her lips puckered ever so slightly. It did things to him God! She had him going from thirty paces. He swallowed and his Adam's apple bobbed up and down. She was tantalizing, teasing and when she wiggled those big juicy breasts ever so slightly, it was causing havoc in his pants.

He considered. How long was it since he'd been with Anita? Too damn long for sure. And by the look of her, this one was hot and ready for any macho male who could do the business with enthusiasm and stamina. Maybe the boy wasn't much good after all. Maybe it would take a stallion like himself to satisfy her.

He started to figure a way out. How could he get her alone without Domingo and Benissimo knowing what he was up to?

But the answer to that was from Domingo himself. When he was somewhat recovered, he strutted across to where the two men lay trussed up. He promptly kicked Clegg in the ribs.

'So, señor, how do you like things now, eh?'

'How do you think, fatso? But don't forget you haven't found that silver yet. You need us so go easy with the boots.'

Domingo squatted. He spat in Clegg's face.

'You and that bastard there know something. Where's your map, señor?' he said, turning to The Deacon who stared stonily at him as if he was deaf. 'Come on you American son of a cow; I don't need use my boots to get the truth out of you. There are other ways...'

His breath sprayed out, pungent with garlic and rotten teeth and The Deacon coughed.

'You'll get nowhere with threats. I didn't survive fifty years without learning a few tricks. When you've been a prisoner of Indians and lived, then you've found out something about yourself.' His own teeth flashed in a smile that was disconcerting. Domingo took off his sombrero and scratched furiously in the region of a biting louse.

'Bull-shit!' he came up with after much thinking. Domingo wasn't a man who could think quickly. He tended to think everyone was like himself. 'Benissimo! What do you think, amigo? Should we try a little persuasion and see if this bastard here is telling the truth? But search them both first. I want that map that he claims he holds,' pointing at The Deacon with his thumb. He watched as Benissimo searched roughly for the map, tearing The Deacon's shirt as he did so.

The Deacon looked down ruefully; 'The only black shirt I've got and I was quite fond of it!'

Clegg smiled as he watched the by-play and felt a well-up of respect for a man who was in a tight corner, and wasn't going to let scum like Domingo faze him. He was also curious. Where the hell had Westerley hidden the damned map? Or was he another who was bluffing? Christ! Maybe they only had the quarter map that he now held. If so, they were up the creek without a paddle, for

Rodriguez' map only showed the last vital clue. It needed the rest to pinpoint the whole.

Then he thought about what he'd done with the map at the first hint of trouble. It might be that Westerley had had the presence of mind too, to stash it. He took heart.

'He's got no map, Domingo,' Benissimo shook his head at Domingo, who stomped up and went and ferreted in the Rodriguez wagon and brought out a bottle of liquor. He pulled the cork and took a long long drink, then sighed.

'Then I don't suppose the other bastard has anything either. I wonder what happened to Rodriguez' map? The old devil was a cunning bastard. Anyhow, enough of wondering. We'll have us a ball. We'll see just how long it takes to make these cursed Americanos sing! Come on, string 'em up to the tail-gate of that wagon over there. We'll haul 'em up shoulder to shoulder so they can take part in the contest. He who shouts first can be stabbed by the other!' He gave a long-drawn-out belly laugh, and Birdie listening at a distance, shuddered. God! How long would it be until this young bug-eyed dollop of shit took his eyes off her tits and did something about the state he was in?

She took a deep breath. She'd noticed a small boulder close by. It was loose. At some time it had been disturbed by a wagonwheel and gouged out of the ground. If she could just stretch out her hand, she could grasp it

'What are you waiting for?' she whispered strongly. Paulo looked at her and then at The Mexican. His face was already pale but now it looked pinched.

'You bitch!' he muttered out of the side of his mouth. 'So soon? You'll take anybody...!'

Birdie's eyes glared. 'You're wrong, Paulo. I'm fighting for our lives.' She switched on a smile as the young Mexican drew near and looked down at her. His mouth worked as if he was hungry.

'What did you say?'

'I said what are you waiting for? You want

me bad, don't you, and you such a strong man with muscular arms and thighs just aching to be caressed. Do you like your thighs caressing, caro?'

He turned and looked back at what was going on more than a hundred yards away. Both men were concentrating on the strung-up prisoners. He swallowed. It would be hours before Domingo and Benissimo were satisfied with what they would be doing, unless the swine died first. He could take her before they even looked around to see what he was doing. His breath came fast. Maybe he could take her, two three times ... he was quite capable. He dropped to his knees and looked at her, at her bound wrists and ankles. He would have to cut her free. But that was no problem. Straddling her, he could bind her up again before she tried any tricks. Besides, he'd have the bitch exhausted before he tied her up.

His mind was made up. His body was ready and he was a slave to his own needs. Hell's teeth! He couldn't get her loosened fast enough. Touching her was bringing a wetness...

His hands trembled as he fumbled with her bonds. He loosed her ankles first as a cautionary measure. He wasn't really worried that she might strike at him. Her breasts were heaving. She was in just such a state as himself. She wanted him. She was a hot-arsed piece of rump...

He freed her hands and then he flung himself down on top of her. His mouth sought hers with such ferocity it left her gasping. Then he was tearing at her clothes, with animal abandon. He growled and all his frustrations boiled up in him. He parted her legs with violence, one hand seeking a buttock while the other held an arm.

Birdie gasped and panicked. This jasper was coming on too strong. If she didn't do something quick, she'd have to endure the whole rotten business; not that she wasn't used to coping with unpleasant characters, but in this case it wasn't ethical. This would be rape. In the past, she'd allowed it as a means of making a living. This was the first time a man was going to have his way without her permission. To hell with that!

She tried kneeing him but it didn't work. He was too heavy. Then he freed her arm to squeeze a breast before biting a nipple and this was her chance She took it.

Stretching out, her fingers closed strongly on the boulder. It was heavy and clumsy and she gritted her teeth as she lifted it and then it crashed down on to his head.

He cursed and rolled free, dazed, convinced he'd been attacked from behind. He turned his head, expecting a raging Domingo.

It was then, Birdie did a real job. His head slammed against the ground with sickening violence. For a moment she closed her eyes to ease her pounding heart. Then she was scrambling up and untying Paulo's knots.

'Come on, we've got to do something quick, or Clegg and The Deacon are finished!'

Six

'Talk! Damn you!' Domingo lifted a ham-like fist and double-slapped The Deacon's cheeks and rocking his head nearly off its shoulders. The head moved loosely. The Deacon's eyes were shut. Then, with difficulty, he raised his head and opened his eyes. It was hard to focus. Blood dribbled from several cuts. He opened his eyes wide.

'Go to hell! I hope you burn!' And then his chin fell on his chest again.

'By God! I'll make them talk!' Domingo strode over and lifted both heads and then let them drop again.

Both had cuts and The Deacon's leg wound was bleeding heavily where Domingo had scraped off the scabs. Both were stripped naked with only tufts of rags which had not come away after the frenzied tearing and rending.

Then Domingo stalked away to pick up his nearly empty bottle. Benissimo sat a little to one side. He was sober and sickened by what he'd already done. These Americanos were hard, tough men and deserved respect. He knew that he himself would not have held out and taken the torture that Domingo had devised.

Clegg, his bones cracking as he hung from his arms, tried to twist his head to look at The Deacon.

'Westerley, can you hear me?'

'I can hear you.'

'How long can you last?'

'Long enough to beat you, you old hound-dog!' He gave a strangled grunt that was supposed to be a laugh. Clegg marvelled.

'You're a helluva guy, Westerley, you've got balls!'

'And so have you but I don't know for how long. See, the bastard's bringing a smoking faggot from the fire.'

'Hell! I never did like burning wood

160

shoved under my arse!'

'What say we lift our legs at the same time and kick him in the balls when he gets near enough? How's your shoulders?'

'Screaming, but they'll take that little bit extra. What about you?'

'I'm screaming all over so it doesn't matter. I'd rather go out with him rolling about in agony. I'd enjoy that...' He tried to grin again.

'We're well-matched. It's a pity to go out and not know who's the better man...'

'Jesus! Is that all you can think of at a time like this? Look out, here he comes!'

They watched from blurred eyes the approach of the grossly fat man. He waddled rather than walked. Benissimo joined him. This was something new. He wondered what it would be like to be barbecued. He'd never seen it done but he knew from tales he heard that it was one of the Apaches' favourite amusements.

Suddenly a shot blasted past Benissimo's head with the hum of an angry hornet. He jumped and cursed as Domingo rolled on to the ground.

'What the hell…?'

It was Domingo who spotted Birdie standing waving the heavy rifle in their general direction. That son of a bitch, Miguel, must have been hypnotized by the woman! That one kept his brains in his pants.

He tried to rise to his knees to crawl away as Birdie took another shot in their direction. It went wild but it had Domingo flattening his arse as near to the ground as possible. Where the hell was the stupid bugger anyway? He should be around somewhere. Then he thought of the youth, Paulo, and ground his teeth. Maybe the young pup had more guts than his father.

He risked a crablike scuttle but found to his horror that he was moving towards Paulo who now appeared to have found himself a shotgun. He was stationary. Domingo saw at a glance that he had Miguel bottled up and the boy looked sick and there was blood and bruises on his head.

162

'Shit!' The whole project was falling apart. Two half-dead Americanos with the secret of the location of the stolen silver, and looking as if they'd prefer to die than reveal it and only two brainless sidekicks who couldn't be trusted to piss on their own!

It was galling to be held up by this slip of a girl, and where was Benissimo? The big ugly bastard had somehow disappeared at the first shot!

Suddenly all hell exploded. Benissimo had rattled his brains and done something without being told. He'd scrambled away and found his handgun and now was trying to shoot the rifle out of the girl's hand.

The girl's shot went wild and Paulo caught Benissimo high in the chest and he went head over heels and twitched and lay still. But now Miguel was up and diving for Paulo's legs and they rolled over and over as Birdie danced up and down with frustration. Then Domingo took a chance and flung himself on Birdie. She went down, the rifle arcing in the air. The wind was knocked out of her and except for her legs thrashing, she was pinned down tighter than a butterfly.

Feeling her writhing body, warm and soft under him, turned the killing rage into something more deadly and bestial. He reached down and bit her lip. She screamed and tried to beat at his chest. He drew his lips back in a wolf s snarl.

'I should kill you, and I will when I finish with you...'

Then to her fascinated gaze, he opened his eyes wide and reared up and looked down at her in amazement. Suddenly drops of blood trickled down and on to her bared breasts. The trickle became a flood and soon she was covered in a pool of sticky blood.

He was choking and his tongue protruded from his mouth in an effort to speak and then she took his weight as he collapsed.

It was then she saw the arrow rammed hard into the middle of his back.

Someone was rolling the great heavy weight from her. She opened her eyes and looked up into the black eyes of an Indian. He was slight and lean and only wore a breech-clout of soft leather. Across the gleaming shoulders were the straps holding quiver and hunting pouch. At his waist hung a business-like hunting knife. On the ground was a well-cared for Winchester. The only colour about him was the red sweatband holding back the long shaggy hair.

She took heart. He wasn't looking at her with that 'lust' look in the eyes.

'You all right?'

She nodded, thankful he knew English.

'Good.' Then he moved away and walked swiftly with that muscled panther move-ment, that only a man of the wild could master. Birdie felt her blood stir and was ashamed.

She watched until he was standing in front of the two sagging bodies and then turned to look for Paulo. He was lying by Miguel. Beside them both was a very dead Benis-simo. The relief was too much. She threw up and thought she was going to die.

Then, kneeling by Paulo she saw he wasn't

dead but only creased by a bullet. She tore a strip from her petticoat and staunched the blood. She would clean it later and apply some of her depleted stock of herbs on it.

'Paulo, wake up. There's an Indian...'

He groaned and opened his eyes. 'What happened? I was scrapping with Miguel when everything went black.'

'I think one of Benissimo's stray bullets caught you. You're lucky; but see, over there, the Indian is cutting Clegg and Mr Westerley down.'

Paulo struggled to sit up and they both watched amazed, for Clegg was clapping the Indian on the shoulder and they were smiling at each other. Then, they watched Clegg fold up and drop to the ground. The Indian caught him and broke his fall. He lay motionless and Birdie had a sudden tight feeling that the Indian had come too late.

The Deacon was in no better shape. He managed to nod when the Indian cut his thongs.

'Thanks ... blood brother ... Clegg...' and

sank into oblivion.

The Indian stood upright and surveyed the two and then he was loping off, rifle in hand to the place where he had hidden and watched part of the drama.

'What the hell? Surely he's not just leaving us?' Birdie muttered, puzzled at the brave's indifference. Paulo groaned and she turned her attention again to him. His scalp wound was bleeding copiously. She set her teeth. She must muster all her strength to tend the three men.

But she was wrong about the Indian. Soon, he was back leading a stocky mountain mustang. He came to her and threw down a skin bag.

'Medicines. I go to get help from the next valley. Apache camp over hill.' He pointed far down the valley towards a purply-blue haze that was a low-lying spur of rock. 'I bring help,' he said again as if Birdie was a child and couldn't understand. She nodded and so he mounted his pony in one graceful stride and then he was riding like the wind.

Birdie wondered who he was and what miracle had made a wild Apache refrain from taking a few scalps.

She remembered Clegg's reaction before he collapsed. Those two must have known each other, she reflected as she bound up Paulo's bloody head again with a clean strip of petticoat.

Then moving over to the two Americanos, she knelt between them. It was a time to choose which to succour first. Instinctively she turned to Clegg, and wondered. Her loyalty should have been with The Deacon. But of the two, she reckoned Clegg the most dangerous as an enemy but more loyal as a friend. The Deacon could be treacherous to his friends. She resolutely opened the leather bag and riffled through its contents, recognizing certain herbs she was familiar with, and some disgusting ointment that smelled of buffalo fat, and went to work on Clegg's wounds.

He opened his eyes and looked at her.

'Birdie...? Was I dreaming?'

'What about, Clegg?'

'Little Elk. Was he here or was it wishful thinking?'

'He was here. He's gone to get help. There's a camp close by.'

He nodded. 'That figures. This is part of the Apache hunting grounds. I wondered whether Buckmaster's blood-brother would turn up when there was some activity in this valley. I was hoping it would be so. The only hope I had.' He grinned weakly and when she finished dressing his wounds, he slipped away but this time into more restful sleep.

She turned to The Deacon who had suffered more than Clegg. He was the one Domingo had concentrated on to get the map. He lay white and gaunt and the drying blood on his face and chest was already turning black and attracting flies. But he was conscious.

'Give me a drink, Birdie so that I may loosen my tongue and thank the good Lord for his salvation.'

Her lips twisted into what she thought was

a grin but it trembled with reaction.

'You should be thanking Little Elk, not your fire and brimstone God.'

'Is that so? Then the good Lord sent him. For His sake, find some whiskey!'

'All in good time, Mr Westerley. You've got some cuts to attend to and by the looks of your chest, that bastard, Domingo stubbed out his cigarillos on you.'

'Yes, by God, he underestimated what he could do. When you've survived Indian fires...' He broke off. 'Never mind about all that. I survived that and this little lot. I'm coming to believe I've got a charmed life.' He grinned. 'I can't see Clegg here, hauling me back to Fort Smith. I've got a lot of fate and fortune to work out yet! What about that drink?'

She sighed. 'Very well. I'll go and see what there is. Domingo sank a lot of it...!'

'Yeh, now, what about Domingo and his crew? Where are they?'

She looked around her and pointed.

'Dead. They'll not trouble us any more.'

'By God! A miracle indeed.' Birdie's eyes lit up with amusement though her lips pulled down at the corners.

'You might say that, but with a little help from Paulo and myself and a lot from the Indian!' The Deacon grunted and lay quietly until she returned with a nearly empty bottle.

'You're lucky. There's a couple of swigs.'

'Jeeze! Is that all? Not enough to fill my belly button!'

'Look, mister, I'm here to treat your wounds, not play at being your barmaid! Now let's get on and make you comfortable before that Indian returns.'

He raised an eyebrow. He noted the mister and not the respectful Mr Westerley. It was the first time she'd actively shown her new dislike of him.

'Seems like I'm not your favourite person any more. What is it, Birdie? Illusions shattered; memories wrecked?'

'Something like that. I'd lived with dreams of a better father-figure than my old man, and now I find out I was wrong. I feel a bit sour, that's all.'

'I'm sorry. I'm just human like the rest of them. I'm no better or worse than Clegg here. Strangely enough we both have our code of standards. They differ a little but not much. Clegg would rather drag a man back to face death or prison, alive, for the money they bring him. I would rather challenge it face to face, and let the best man go free.' He looked at the sleeping Clegg reflectively. 'It will come to that with us eventually. I'll kill him, or he will take me back.' He grinned mirthlessly. 'And believe me, I've never yet been taken back.'

Birdie was saved answering as a small cavalcade came slowly over the skyline. It was well-strung out. Two travois, half a dozen Indians walking, with Little Elk on his mustang leading the way, and just behind him a small pony carrying a dumpy fat squaw who had a bundle clutched tightly to her bosom.

They finally reached the little group. Little

Elk looked down at them.

'How are they?' His black eyes stared hard at Birdie. She recognized the look that all strangers gave her, an appraising, assessing look. But this time it did not give her a thrill. Her mind was on Paulo and his ambition to take over his grandfather's rancho. This was not an opportunity to be missed. She wanted to be married and respectable. Also, and she hugged this secret to herself, she might be with child ... Paulo's child.

'They'll live,' she answered succinctly and turned away from those black eyes.

She went back to Paulo. He was lying watching the Indians. She smiled.

'They're friendly. The one on the horse knows Clegg.'

Little Elk was a good organizer and soon he had them ready to depart. Clegg roused himself to talk and told him the reason they were entering the valley; He nodded.

'I know the entrance to the old mine. This trail was once the main mule trail. Now it is seldom used for we Apache think this valley is accursed. Spirits of the massacred soldiers still walk. You can hear their voices in the wind...'

'We have a map. We understand the silver was cached somewhere in the valley, for other soldiers came, before the outlaws could get the mule-train out of the valley.'

Little Elk nodded. 'All were killed but two. It has been talked about over the lodge fires, many times. But how did you know about this?'

Clegg glanced at The Deacon.

'He got a map from a prisoner he became friendly with in the pen. The man died but gave him the map. The trouble was, it was not complete. Another held the other piece.'

Little Elk nodded. 'That would be so. White men do not trust each other. For Buckmaster's sake, and because you also are a blood-brother of the Apache, we shall take you to the opening of the old silver mine. But you will have to look for the cache yourselves.' He smiled. 'Our old folk know where it is, but they will not tell us young bucks. The old ones reckon silver is a white man's greed. They do not wish us to become like them.'

Clegg nodded. He knew how the Indians reasoned. Their viewpoint was very different to the white man's. Buffalo and good hunting and full bellies made them rich. They wanted nothing more. These mountain Apache were very different to those who lived on the fringe of civilization as the white man saw it. He and Buckmaster had held long conversations about the red men. After all, Buckmaster should know. He'd lived with them for many years.

Finally they arrived at an overgrown clearing. It was a small flat plain gradually building up to a comparatively low hill. Great boulders were strewn around as if scattered by a giant hand.

The travois stopped and so did the wagons and Birdie looked out. She could see nothing of any man-made earthworks or any sign of any past activity.

'This is it?'

Little Elk, riding alongside the wagon heard her.

'Yes. What did you expect? A mine in running order?'

'No, but I thought there would be signs...'

'Long gone. You see those mesquite bushes over there?' His arm pointed in a long sweep.

'Yes, I see them.'

He smiled. 'The opening is behind those mesquite thorns. Will you brave them?'

Birdie opened her eyes wide.

'Why should we? We're looking for a cache of silver in boxes or bags or however the ore was shipped out, not looking for the mine opening.'

He laughed, showing white teeth. 'If you want water, there is no other known source in the valley. It is one of the reasons we Apache will not hunt in this valley. It would mean taking water from the spirits and we will not do that.'

'Hell! Do you mean we'll have to hack a way through that lot?'

'Yes, if you would live long enough to

climb out of the valley with a heavy load.'

'Will you not help?'

Little Elk shrugged. 'I would not ask my people. Clegg will know what to do.'

'But...'

'We have brought plenty of water to last until Clegg and the man with him are recovered. You need not worry. You will not have to fetch water.' He smiled, knowing what had been in her mind. 'You will have your day occupied in feeding and tending them until they can do for themselves.'

And so it was. At first the old fat squaw examined all three men and treated each one. Then she showed Birdie how to make a soup with which to feed them when they recovered a little. Huge slices of raw liver were chopped up and the sufferers encouraged to swallow the red jelly-like substance. It would promote energy and sustenance. It was always the first thing taken from a dead animal and eaten warm dripping with blood by the hunters who had probably not eaten for twenty-four hours and been long on their unsaddled ponies. Liver gave strength to endure.

The feeding of the liver made Birdie feel sick but the smell of the soup, thick with wild onions and fennel and slivers of meat scraped from the bones of an elk soon made her nose twitch. She was hungry and hollow in the belly. The old woman smiled and put a hand on her stomach.

'Mother must feed well and keep up strength. Eat liver too!'

'How ... how did you know?' The old woman smiled a secret smile.

'Old Moonflower know, she always knows when new baby made! It is the look in the eyes.' She turned away to pack her herbs and medicines.

Paulo, lying a few feet away during this exchange, tugged at Birdie's tattered skirt.

'What was the old squaw talking about?'

Birdie looked at Paulo consideringly. He was young and innocent and she much older by her way of life, and she wondered at his reaction. She'd figured on waiting until they got back to the rancho. He was young to have the responsibility. Still ... what was done, was done and by God, she was going to fight to better herself and the life of her baby. She could control Paulo

'I'm having a baby.'

'You what?' Paulo's jaw dropped.

'You heard. I'm having a baby.'

'Whose?' Birdie's eyes fired up in anger, but she was wary. It could be Clegg's...

'Yours, of course. Who else? I haven't been with anyone since you straddled me. You know that.' He looked at her with suspicion.

'I don't know whether I do know. It could have happened...'

She smacked his face and his head rocked back.

'Are you saying I two-timed you?'

'Now, look here, Birdie, I'm not saying...'

'Well, say what you mean! It's yours and there's an end of it.'

He swallowed. 'I'm sorry, but you know what you are...'

'Go on, don't be shy, say it! I was a whore,

but I'm not any more.' Suddenly she started to cry, and though his head was still pounding, Paulo struggled upright and gathered her in his arms.

'I'm sorry. I'm just a blundering fool. We'll get married and we'll build up the rancho together. It even might be fun having a baby. My son! Yes, it could be good.'

'I don't know why I'm crying like this. I never cry,' she wept.

'Now that's all right. If you want to cry, you cry.' The crying made him feel big and protective. He patted her back and then kissed her. Yes, it would be good having a wife like Birdie and keeping her in check, and every now and again showing her who was boss…

Seven

A week passed before Clegg and The Deacon were their usual selves. The cuts were healing but the bruising remained, giving them an ugly look of menace. Paulo was still pale. He had suffered a bout of concussion and for one night Birdie had been frightened. It had been that night which made her realize how much the youth meant to her.

Each morning they had found a couple of jack-rabbits, a young buck or a haunch of meat waiting for them at their camp-fire. The Apaches had come and gone without a whisper of sound. It reminded them all of how vulnerable they would be against the whole tribe. They were all silently grateful for Clegg's connection with the Apache.

The Deacon went about the chores of the camp, planning what they should do next.

181

He ruminated on showing his map to Clegg. It wasn't going to be easy if Clegg didn't offer to show Rodriguez' portion.

On the seventh day he made up his mind.

'We've got to get in there and get fresh water,' he said, nodding to the barrier of mesquite between them and the expected mine opening. 'I understand it is close by.'

'Yeh, I've been waiting for you to bring up the subject. Ready to tackle that mesquite?' Clegg was being casual. He chewed on a piece of tough grass.

'As I'll ever be. What water's left in the barrels on the wagons is bad and flyblown. We'll never get out without fresh water.'

'Then that's it. We'll give Paulo a shout. That is if we can prise him away from Birdie,' Clegg grinned. 'What it is to be young and in love!'

'She's pregnant, did you know?'

Clegg frowned. 'No, I didn't. what of it anyway?'

'Look, I've been a bastard nearly all my life, I admit it and I haven't really been what you might call kind to her. She's always made me uncomfortable, what with her jumped up idea of me. Making me out to be some kind of bloody saint! But I want her and the boy to have a chance. Besides...' he hesitated, 'I think you and I have some unfinished business.'

Clegg gave him a long slow look. 'Yeh ... I was hoping you would suggest it. Mind you, in other circumstances you and I could have been pards. As it is ... we're pulling two ways at once. But it would be nice to settle it once and for all.' Clegg grinned and chewed faster.

'We'll lay down the rules. When I kill you, I'll bury you deep so the coyotes don't dig you up. I'll share with Paulo and Birdie.'

'You're wrong there, Westerley. I'm going to kill you and bury you deep and to hell with the bounty! But first we got to find that silver.'

'Yeh, I was coming to that. I vote we both produce the pieces of map and find the cache and send those two lovebirds on their way with their share and one of the wagons. We don't need witnesses for what we're going to do.'

Clegg scratched his chin.

'If you're thinking of a doublecross...'

'I'm a bastard, but not that kind. I've never been a bushwhacker. I want to kill you in a fair fight. Eyeball to eyeball ... legs spread and hands a-quivering to go. What d'you say?'

'That's the way it should be, or we'll never know.' Clegg held out his hand. 'I never thought I'd shake the hand of a wanted man.'

'As to that, I never thought I'd shake the hand of a goddamn bounty-hunter.'

They suddenly grinned at each other. Clegg squared his shoulders.

'Right! Let's get that randy young stallion prised from his woman and get started. It'll take a day to cut through that damned mesquite and another to open up the spring and I'm getting thirstier by the minute!'

He was wrong. It took three days and

numerous cuts and curses. Birdie helped in her small way and each night dropped down asleep on her feet. Then at last the nightmare was over. The rotted frame of the tunnel leading into the mine was revealed and a cluster of scrub and gamma grass betrayed the presence of water a dozen yards to the left.

The spring was choked and it took time to dig down deep to find it but at last they came to a seepage enough to fill a stetson, and when it was ladled out, the hole slowly filled again.

'Yippee!' Paulo tossed his straw hat into the air and grabbed Birdie about the waist. 'We've done it! We can fill the barrels for the return journey. All we have to do now is find the silver!' His eyes glistened, his head wound forgotten. He seemed taller and more confident and older. The Americans smiled with him.

The Deacon coughed. 'We've got to find the cache yet.'

Paulo's expressive face clouded over.

'Oh, we'll find it, never fear. We've got both pieces of map, boy.' The Deacon grinned. 'We're letting you go back on your own. A kind of honeymoon if you like. Clegg here is going to ask Little Elk for an escort for you. They'll be no trouble to you. They'll remain high on the mountains but they'll watch over you until you're well past the Rio Grande and at the border of their territory.'

'But aren't you two coming with us?' Birdie looked from one to the other. 'Clegg, what's the idea?'

'Like the man said, you're having a honeymoon.'

'We've had that already,' Birdie said sharply. 'There's something else, isn't there?' Again she looked at them. 'Don't tell me you're reckoning on a shootout!'

'Aw, shut your bitching face!' The Deacon snarled, 'You're a nosy cow. I should have let your paw belt you! He must have had some good reason for wanting to!'

Birdie's mouth dropped open. There was

186

such pain in her that it was likely to strangle her.

The Deacon turned away. He couldn't bear to watch the pain he was inflicting. He cursed inwardly. Why should he have to kill her illusions? She was nothing but a whore anyway...

Clegg watched in silence. He thought he understood. Westerley didn't want Birdie agonizing over him. He wanted to cut her right out of his life and make her glad to lose her girlish dreams. Free her from all memories.

'Come on,' he said gruffly to Westerley, 'let's go and find that cache.'

They moved out with all the spare horses. If they found the cache they would need those horses to carry the loads. They also took their weapons and all the lariats from both wagons, and two spades. They expected to have to dig.

They were gone for a day and a half. It had been a long hard time. Birdie had busied herself in making hardtack pan bread that would keep on the journey. Little Elk, who seemed to know the Americanos' every movement came and dropped down a leather pouch. It contained strips of jerky. He smiled at her and nodded. 'Soon, you will be on your journey. I have talked to Clegg up there, and he has asked a favour. You need not worry. Some of my braves will escort you from a distance. It is arranged.'

'Thank you. You are very kind.'

Little Elk bowed his head in a dignified silence and then crossed his chest with his fist.

'I go now. I will not return.'

'Then it's goodbye. I'll never forget you.'

'Or I, you!' Was there something in his eyes? Birdie couldn't decide. Anyway, it didn't matter any more. She had Paulo and the promise of a new life on his rancho. To be mistress instead of becoming a beat-up old-before-her-time whore wearing too much paint on her face to hide the ravages that coarse men would put on her. Then there was the prospect of the baby. She too hoped it would be a boy...

Paulo's shout interrupted her reverie. She ran to him and he put an arm about her waist.

'Look up there, see ... there's a movement. It's Clegg and The Deacon and the horses!'

'Where? Where? I can't see them.'

'Over there, just past that needle-like peak of rock. See? Those moving black dots.'

'Are you sure? It might be the Indians.'

'No, by God! They don't ride like that all out in the open and those horses are moving slowly as if they're loaded to their hocks!' His voice was high with excitement. He looked down and kissed her. 'Tomorrow, love, we'll be on our way home!'

Soon, all doubts were gone. She could see clearly the Americanos on their horses and the heavy laden pack-horses coming slowly behind. Birdie rushed to the fire and built it up and began boiling up the mush of beans and the remains of two jackrabbits. They would be hungry for some home-cooking.

The smell of fresh brewed coffee greeted

them on arrival. Both men were grinning. Birdie wanted to rush forward and fling her arms about Clegg. She restrained herself however for The Deacon had a nasty temper, and though he had devastated her with his cutting remarks she wanted to give him no excuse to start on Clegg.

The situation between the two men still worried her. She still hoped she might change their minds.

'So we've done it,' Clegg's face showed nothing of what was to come. 'You're going to be rich, Paulo,' he said to the silent youth. 'You can make an honest woman of Birdie and give her all the things she's never been used to.'

Paulo nodded. 'I'll do that and all. You know we're having a baby?'

Clegg smiled. 'Yeh, smart-arse here told me. It seems he knows about these things. So, you'll be on your way tomorrow.'

'Not without you,' Birdie broke in. 'You've done all the hard work, locating the silver. It only seems fair we should go out together.'

Clegg's eyes went cold and hard. Birdie shivered. He looked just like The Deacon when he'd clammed up. There was nothing to choose between them. She wondered why she cared what happened to either of them. Paulo was the kind of man she could love. Warm and kind and gentle, with no coldness in the eyes, no killer's eyes...

'Was the cache hard to find?'

The Deacon laughed. 'Mossman and Rodriguez weren't very original. It was easy to find when one had the map and knew the silver was there for the finder. Of course if you weren't looking for it, you could pass right by it. It was buried under a lone dead tree with a boulder rolled in front of it. The boulder looked as if it had a tree growing out of its top. All revealed when the two pieces of map were put together. The worst was digging it out and setting it on the backs of those horses. The blamed critturs are not used to carrying loads. Anyhow, we're here in a piece. Tomorrow we load both wagons and fill the water barrels and we take our own horses and leave the spare horses for Little Elk for all his trouble. We've seen him and made arrangements...'

'Yes. He came and told us and brought us a supply of jerky.'

'He did, did he? He's a good leader, is Little Elk. He thinks of details. Now what about this here supper? I could eat my horse!'

That night Birdie was too excited to sleep. When the moon was high and casting dark blue shadows she looked outside the wagon and saw the glow of the small fire and the two Americanos sitting shoulder to shoulder talking low. As she watched, Clegg laughed and some of the tension went out of her. Maybe they had buried their differences out there hunting that silver together.

The next morning they were all up early and the camp was struck.

'So you are coming with us?' Birdie's heart was singing. Both men looked relaxed.

'Nope! You go on ahead. The second wagon will catch you up.'

Birdie looked from one to the other. 'You

didn't say *we*. You said the wagon! That means only one of you is coming.' Suddenly she was weeping and she flung herself into Clegg's arms. 'For God's sake, what kind of fools are you? There's enough silver for both of you. Why not just take it and go? You can both be rich!'

'You don't understand. A woman never would.' Clegg held her tightly and then bent and kissed her on the mouth.

'Thanks Birdie. I'm sorry we never got it together again, but really a bounty-hunter isn't the kind of man a girl should latch on to. Paulo's a good boy and he'll make a good man. You're lucky, girl. Don't gamble away your luck. Here, Paulo, catch her and look after her or by God, I'll be coming after you!'

Then he threw her up into the wagon beside Paulo who was waiting. He hauled her beside him and held her struggling while he pulled on the reins with the other.

'So long, fellers,' he bawled. 'We'll see you at the rancho!'

'You fool, Paulo! We won't see them. They're going to kill each other!' Paulo laughed.

'No they won't. They might try but both are too fly to catch it!'

The two men watched the wagon gather pace and move ahead. Somewhere in those hills, the Apache would watch the rate of progress from their hidden places. Clegg was confident that nothing would happen to the wagon, its owners, or the fortune in silver. It would get through.

He felt strangely light-hearted. It wasn't often he could help a young couple get their feet firmly on a rosy path. He was sorry he hadn't asked Birdie to name the boy after him. Still, Percy wasn't such a good name. A kid had to be tough to live up to it. It hadn't done him any harm when he was a kid. The fights he got into because of it had toughened him. Still ... he wished he'd been called Bill or Tom. Anyhow, she wouldn't call him Clegg, that was for sure.

He was smiling when he turned to The Deacon.

'Well? When is it to be?'

The Deacon eyed him. 'Are you sure you want to go ahead? You could be dead by sundown.'

'I'm sure. Not getting cold feet? If you are, I'll just take you in, in lieu.'

'Now balls to that! I just feel reluctant about killing you. We've become what we might call friends during these last few weeks...'

'Speak for yourself,' snorted Clegg. 'We're too much alike to be friends.'

'Then that's it then. I'm ready when you are.'

'Sure, what about now before we eat. No need to waste good food.'

'Right. What about over there? No shadows and the sun giving us equal advantage.'

Both men strode out, checking guns as they went. Clegg glanced sideways at The Deacon.

'One gun or two?'

'One. I don't need more than one to send you to kingdom-come.'

'Likewise!' They glared at each other as the adrenalin started to rise.

The old familiar feeling of meanness stole across Clegg, freezing nerves and thoughts to the job in hand.

The Deacon was going through a similar experience. His brain was icing up. He was only aware of his eyes and his right hand. He found himself flexing his fingers, his eyes unblinking as they watched every tremble, every movement of Clegg beside him.

Then when they were mutually agreed that this was the place, they moved back to back, with nothing else being said. Both had taken part in deliberate duelling before. It was nothing new, but this time it was different, each was facing a man as good as himself ... or maybe a touch better. The sweat broke out on both of them. At the last moment, both experienced a brief doubt...

'Ten paces and then turn and shoot,' The Deacon called.

'Right! One ... two ... three...' And so they counted together and as if by magic both hesitated on the count often.

But both whirled into the standard gun-man's crouch at the same time, gun in hand and exploding at the same time.

High on the rimrock, Little Elk sat his mustang, watching. He saw the Americanos striding out, and then turning and firing. He saw the puffs of blue smoke and he watched both men blasted backwards like the grotesque stuffed straw dolls that the girls of his tribe liked to cuddle.

He would never understand why two strong men could take pleasure in killing each other. He was concerned. If they were both dead, then there would be two more restless spirits to haunt this accursed valley. He picked his way down from the summit until he came to a narrow trail and then he made better time. If they were dead he would bury them and help to appease their souls...

Clegg opened his eyes and found himself

spreadeagled and staring up into a relentless sun. What the hell ... he had a throbbing head and a burn on his arm that had brought him round. He tried to raise his head and saw that The Deacon lay some yards from him. He was still. So the bastard was dead and he was still alive! He tried to grin but the pain was coming in waves. The bugger had got him through the upper shoulder, his right shoulder no less. Then he remembered his vow to bury The Deacon deep. He was going to have a hell of a job with that bloody arm. He set his teeth. A promise was a promise. He'd have to do it even if it took him a week.

He turned over on to his belly with an effort and then pulled up his knees. He would have to crawl over and see what damage had been done. So he started to crawl and cursed as he did so. The cursing kept him going.

The Deacon lay on his stomach. He couldn't move but he watched Clegg make his agonizing crawl. He was disappointed. So one gun hadn't been enough after all? Well, it figured. That had been a mistake. He'd not taken into account that Clegg was superior to all the others he'd shot in the back, front and from above. He didn't have Clegg's fancy ideas about honour. It had only been curiosity to find out which of them was the king-spot that kept him from shooting Clegg in the back. That, and the damned strange feeling that he and Clegg should never meet.

Now it was too late. There was blood dripping from his side. The bastard hadn't shot to kill, or if he had he'd made a bloody balls-up of it. He couldn't see Clegg's hand trembling at the crucial moment.

He could feel blood dripping. Christ it was pouring out of him. He was bleeding like a stuck pig. There was no pain. That would come later. He just felt numb and helpless. Hell! He had to do something. He couldn't expect Clegg to do all the crawling. He might as well help out.

He dragged up his knees under him and slithered more than crawled along the ground.

He heard Clegg's shout of anger.

'So, you bastard, you're still alive!'

The Deacon heaved himself another few inches.

'Yeh, I'm not dead yet, Clegg. What are you going to do about it?'

Clegg gasped and crawled until he was within a few feet of The Deacon. If both held out their hands they could nearly touch. They would do so, with another mighty effort.

They lay so that they could look into each other's eyes. Both saw the sweat of uncertainty in the other.

'I could do with a drink,' The Deacon rasped, his dry lips drawn back in a snarl.

'Would it make you more prepared to meet that good Lord of yours?' Clegg couldn't resist asking.

'Shit! I just want a drink for a drink's sake. How about you? What do you want?'

'I want to know whether you told the truth about Molly. I want to know whether you told me a load of bullshit or whether she was two-timing me. Which was it, Westerley?'

Steve Westerley laughed. 'Funny about that. I really didn't want to tell you about her. As much as I hated you ... and feared you, I didn't want to hurt you. I figured you had your dreams too. I seem to have the knack of wrecking illusions...'

'For Chrissake, don't give me all that high-falutin' crap! In a few hours you and me will be forking our horses in the sky and I want to know. *Was she that kind of girl you said she was?*'

Westerley sighed. 'She was. I'll be facing my Lord soon and I tell you she was. Can I say fairer than that Clegg, old man? Killing her folks was just a reaction after she screamed rape because I turned her down. She was frightened of what the preacher man would say to the good folk of Twofork Creek, and I was frightened of the reactions of those same good folk. So I shot them all in panic. The good Lord forgive me.'

Clegg nodded. 'Well, we'll both know whether He forgives you in a few hours. It'll be either the sun or the wounds which will do the trick.'

The Deacon stretched out his hand.

'Will you shake? Somehow it doesn't matter any more.'

Clegg gasped and then smiled grimly. 'Why not? As you say it doesn't matter any more.' He struggled a little and then their fingers touched. Both smiled at the other, sweat heavy on upperlips and running down foreheads. The Deacon gasped.

'The pain's coming now. You're a bloody bad shot...'

'And so are you. You should have killed me...' Then they were lying quietly as if they slept, clasping hands like pards.

Little Elk drew up beside them and slipped off his horse and taking his waterskin, poured water liberally down each throat. Both men were alive, which was a miracle indeed. Maybe the Great Spirit didn't want any more unhappy spirits wandering this valley.

Little Elk examined the wounds. Both were bad but not bound to be fatal. He stood up and raising his hands to his mouth, made the call of a mating wolf. He called again and again and then at last he got a reply.

Now all he could do was squat on his heels and wait. He smiled and looked up into the clear blue sky. Somewhere up there was the Great Spirit, and it could be his wish that the two Americanos would have to live together for quite some time and if that were so, they might solve their differences. It would be a good thing. Yes, even a man like The Deacon could become a blood-brother just as Clegg had done. It would be good for the Apache to have the allegiance of these men as well as that of the great Buckmaster.

These men were worth saving. He would instruct Moonflower that she must do her best for it would be for the honour of the tribe...

Little Elk lay back and dreamed. Some day this particular remnant of the Apache tribe would be rich and powerful again. Maybe these two men might be persuaded to stay. They could become partners and the silver they'd taken from the ground used for the benefit of all. He smiled. Maybe the great Spirit might take all those restless spirits back up into the ancient hunting grounds and then they could use that source of new water...

His eyes glowed. He lay back and dreamed his dreams. Some day he would be regarded as a great chief...

The publishers hope that this book has given you enjoyable reading. Large Print Books are especially designed to be as easy to see and hold as possible. If you wish a complete list of our books please ask at your local library or write directly to:

Dales Large Print Books
Magna House, Long Preston,
Skipton, North Yorkshire.
BD23 4ND